THE MAN AT WINDMERE

ALSO BY VELDA JOHNSTON

THE MAN
AT
WINDMERE

a novel of suspense

by
Velda Johnston

Dodd, Mead & Company
New York

No part of this book may be reproduced in any form
without permission in writing from the publisher.
Published by Dodd, Mead & Company, Inc.
71 Fifth Avenue, New York, N.Y. 10003
Manufactured in the United States of America
Text design by Maryanne DeMarco
Text set in Caledonia
First Edition

1   2   3   4   5   6   7   8   9   10

Library of Congress Cataloging-Publication Data

Johnston, Velda.
    The man at Windmere.

    I. Title.
PS3560.0394M26   1988   813'.54   88-16233
ISBN 0-396-09372-8

This one is for Joan Monticone

THE MAN AT WINDMERE

1

Maryann Fallon first saw Windmere, standing beside its lake in a cup of low hills, near dusk of a spring evening. Despite the fading light, its gray stone walls and tall white porch pillars were still visible. Lamp glow fell through long windows onto a white mist hovering above the water. From the hillside path along which the jolting farm cart carried her, Maryann could see smoke rising from many chimneys into the crisp air.

For a moment she let herself imagine what would be awaiting her if that house, rather than her mother-in-law's farm, had been her destination. Crackling fires. Delicious food. A soft bed. And before bed, a long, soaking bath to wash away the accumulated fatigue of a journey that seemed endless.

It was just a fancy. It never occurred to her that she would enter that house someday. Even less did she imagine that she would find there, not only crystal goblets and long ancestral portraits, but what the Germans call a *doppel-gänger*, an evil reverse image of everything precious and beloved that she had lost.

"What house is that?"

The old man on the driver's seat did not turn. He said in the Yorkshire accent that sounded like an aged echo of Donald's voice, "That be Windmere."

"Whose house is it?"

"Sir Rodney Athaire's."

"Who is he?"

"Baronet."

The old man did not elaborate. But then, he had been sullen and uncommunicative ever since that afternoon, when a porter at Leeds Station had dragged him, surly and more than a little drunk, from a nearby pub. He had not been too drunk, though, to demand three shillings from Maryann for the journey into the Pennine Hills.

The cart creaked on through the gathering dark. She had been riding with both hands clutching the cart's edges to ease its jolting, but now she used her left hand to draw her red wool shawl more closely about her. Although the night wasn't really cold, she found it so. But then, she had felt cold at intervals ever since the day her life had stopped.

Yes, stopped. She was twenty-seven, and her life was over.

Oh, there was still Jaimie back there in Connecticut. But the long years stretching ahead of her would be lived not for her own sake but for him, the little scrap of himself that Donald had left upon this earth.

She checked her thoughts. Self-pity was a luxury she could not afford. She was thousands of miles from the only home she had ever known, on her way to meeting two women she had never seen. She must keep thinking of ways to make herself so useful to them, and so agreeable, that six months from now, or a year, or whenever small Jaimie was strong enough for the journey, they would say, "Why, of course you must bring him here."

Some sort of ruin up on the hilltop to her right, its arches black against what was left of the daylight. She said, "What is that up there?"

"What it looks like. Old abbey ruins."

"How did it become a ruin?"

"Old Harry's men did it."

After a moment she realized that he must mean King Henry VIII. It had been more than three hundred years since Henry, in his war against the Roman Church, had looted and razed many English monasteries. And yet this old man spoke as if it had happened only recently. Maryann suddenly felt very American, very aware that hers was a country so young that now, in 1857, there were still quite a few people who could remember the inauguration of George Washington.

She realized that they must be in the Pennines now. The road, growing rougher, dipped, rose, dipped again. On either side were low stone walls, sometimes half hidden by bushes or trees. Beyond the walls were meadows, dotted with white shapes that she knew must be grazing sheep. And beyond the meadowland the outline of hills stood black against a moonless but star-brilliant sky. Now and then she heard the hooting of owls, and once a bird she presumed to be some sort of nighthawk flew across the road, only inches beyond the head of the spavined horse, so close that Maryann could hear the rustle of its wings.

A few times she saw farmhouses, some dark, some with

3

lamplight falling from their windows. She thought of what must be going on in those houses. Wives washing up the supper dishes—only over here, Donald had said, farmers and working-class people called the final meal of the day tea. Husbands would be enjoying a last pipe beside a dying fire. Perhaps in one of the houses parents bent over the cradle of a sick child. And perhaps in some of the darkened houses couples lay entwined—

But she would not think of love, of kisses in the night, or of the weight of Donald's long lean body. Love was part of her stopped life, her life that had ended the moment she saw him lying in the road, his blue eyes holding a fixed stare of outrage that told her he had known he was about to die, about to leave the life he had found so sweet.

Some sort of blossoms made a white blur now and then among the trees and bushes along the low walls. A fragrance filled the air. White lilac? Perhaps.

The creaking cart turned onto a narrower road. Surely they must be near the journey's end. Donald had told her that the Fallon farm was less than six hours by horse and cart from Leeds, but it seemed to her that they had been traveling twice that long already.

Something odd about the meadows on either side of this narrow road. After a while she realized what it was. No tinkle of collar bells, no white, grazing shapes. But surely this road must lead to the Fallon farm, and surely Donald had told her that it was a sheep farm.

At the same time she began to be aware of a smell, heavy, all-pervasive, at once sweetish and sourish. She felt her stomach turn.

"What is that *smell*?"

The driver chuckled. "Pigs. Pigs and pig swill."

"Pigs!"

"You said you be Flora Fallon's sister-in-law, didn't you? Young Donald's widow?" He sounded as if he were enjoying himself.

"Yes."

"You didn't know she switched from sheep to pigs?"

"No."

"Well, she did, last autumn. Figured there'd be more profit in it, since nobody else around here raises pork. May be right, too, from what I hear." It was his longest speech of the journey.

"Does the smell—"

"Does the smell what?"

"Is it always this bad?"

"Aye. But you'll get used to it."

She could see the pigs now. Or at least she could see, on either side of the road, pens where dark shapes grunted and sometimes squealed. In the starlight their hides were faintly luminous.

The road curved. Up ahead, set in a rectangle of bare earth, was a farmhouse of what appeared to be gray stone, its windows dark. "Here you be," the driver said.

Maryann fought down her disappointment over the dark, unwelcoming windows. After all, the two Fallon women had no way of knowing the day, or even the week, of her arrival. In Boston, before going aboard the brig *Western Star*, she had dispatched a letter to them by one of the few remaining clipper ships. But even so, they could not be sure when her slower sailing brig would reach Liverpool, nor how long it would take her to find transportation to this isolated farm in the West Riding.

Grunting, the driver got to the ground. He let down the

5

cart's tailgate. Then, not stopping to help his passenger to the ground, he walked to the farmhouse door, pounded on it, waited, pounded again. Stiffly, Maryann slid out of the cart, turned, and grasped the handles of her portmanteau. She was standing beside the driver when light bloomed behind the small square panes of the windows.

The door opened. A woman in a brown woolen robe stood there, holding an oil lamp at about shoulder height.

Donald had told Maryann that his sister was four years his senior. That would make her thirty-six now. But this woman, with her gaunt face between two braided falls of gray-brown hair, looked ten years older than that, or even more.

The driver said, "Here she be, clear from America."

Flora's first words were to the cartman, not to her sister-in-law. "You got your pay?"

"Aye."

"Then good night to you." Her eyes, grayish blue, moved to Maryann. "Come in."

Maryann walked inside. She had a swift impression of a stone floor, of wooden benches flanking a wide fireplace, a rectangular oak table with straight chairs pulled up to it, a rocking chair in one corner, ladderlike stairs leading to a loft. At first she thought there was only the one big room. Then she saw that there was a half-open door in the rear wall and two closed ones on the right-hand wall.

Everything looked very clean, and yet the smell was there. Not as overwhelming as it had been outside, but still there.

"Flora! What's happening, Flora?"

The voice came from beyond one of the doors in the right-hand wall. Undoubtedly the voice of Flora's mother

6

—Flora's and Donald's. A look of annoyance crossed Flora's face. Obviously she wished her brother's widow had arrived at an earlier hour.

"It's Donald's wife, Ma!" Then, in a lower voice. "You'll have to see her, now she's woke up. Better put your portmanteau down."

Maryann, who hadn't realized she was still holding it, set her portmanteau on the floor. She followed Flora into a small room. A woman lay in a double bed with a headboard of unvarnished oak. Despite her wrinkles and the white hair showing around the edges of her frilly nightcap, the lively expression in her blue eyes made her seem oddly youthful.

"Donald's wife." The woman smiled, and then Maryann knew where Donald had got his smile—that warm, gentle smile that always had the power to twist her heart.

She had known from Donald that Mrs. Fallon was bed-ridden. Something had gone wrong with her spine about ten years before.

"My grandson!" Mrs. Fallon said. "How was he when you left him?"

"Stronger. The doctor said that in time he will be quite sturdy again."

"Oh, I do hope that he'll be strong enough to stand the journey soon. I want to see him before I die."

"Now stop that foolish talk about dying!" Flora's voice was sharp. "You're going to be like your own ma. You'll live to be ninety, bad back and all. Now go back to sleep."

Maryann smiled at her mother-in-law and then followed Flora into the main room. Flora said, "You ate on the way here?"

"Yes." Around five the cart driver had stopped at an inn.

In its smoke-blackened main room he had joined a group of roughly clad men, perhaps farmers or sheep-drovers or both. She had sat at a table in one corner eating shepherd's pie and trying to ignore the snickers and covert stares from the other tables.

"Good thing you're not hungry. As you see, the fire's out. This time of year I don't bank it." She paused. "I suppose you'll be wanting your bed."

"Yes, please. I'm very tired." Picking up her portmanteau, she turned toward the ladderlike stairs.

"Not up there. Donald's bed used to be up there, but I moved it. I needed the loft to store sorghum and rye. Takes more than swill to raise pigs, you know."

The pigs. Tomorrow she would ask questions about the pigs. "Then where—"

"When I got your letter, I moved Donald's bed into the storeroom beyond the pantry."

She turned toward the door in the rear wall. Without being bidden to do so, Maryann followed. Flora led her through a narrow pantry. Maryann noticed a wheel of cheese, crocks of varying sizes, loaflike shapes wrapped in cloth. Then she stood in a small, low-ceilinged room furnished with a single bed, a straight chair, and a stand holding a basin and pitcher of plain white crockery.

Beside the pitcher was the stub of a candle in a metal holder. Flora set down the lamp, picked up a flint box, and lit the candle stub. "Not much there, but the light should last until you're undressed. Now, there's a chamber pot under the bed. Or you can go through the back door there to the privy. Well, good night."

8

2

In the room next to her mother's, Flora stared up into the darkness. Donald's widow had been a disappointment to her. In spite of knowing that Maryann was what folks called gently raised—a parson's daughter, in fact—Flora had hoped she might turn out to be a big buxom girl, someone who might be of real use on a farm. Instead, here was this spindly thing with a coil of dark hair that looked too heavy for her small head and long neck and dark eyes that looked too big for her face. But these skinny ones could surprise you. She'd seen some who could outwork women almost twice their weight.

And anyway, she thought grimly, *this* one was going to work. It was only because she needed help that she had consented to Maryann's coming here. Of course, she would have preferred a man. But here in the West Riding, where nearly everyone raised sheep, it was hard to find men to work on a pig farm. What made it even harder was that many young Yorkshiremen chose to work in the Lancashire knitting mills, or—the Lord only knew why—the West Riding coal mines, with their threat of quick death by cave-in or slow death by lung disease.

One thing no young man had chosen to do, ever, was to ask her to marry. Somehow she had known, even as a very young girl, that no man would. She didn't know why not. True, she was plain, but girls equally plain got husbands. Perhaps there was something about her that frightened men. Perhaps they sensed in her a will to succeed that was more steely than any of them possessed.

Certainly she was determined to succeed with her pigs. It seemed to her an excellent time for the venture. With cheap, slave-raised cotton from the southern United States pouring into England, some of the woolen mills were being converted into producers of cotton fabrics. That made sheep raising less profitable.

If everything went well—if swine fever didn't strike and if the slaughterhouse didn't raise its fees for butchering and curing to exorbitant heights—she would soon be selling Fallon farm ham and bacon for miles around. If she grew richer as the sheep farmers grew poorer, she could buy up their land to raise more pigs. Someday she would be a rich woman, able to look down on those who had held her of little account because she was plain and the daughter of an illiterate mother, and of a father who had deserted his family.

And it was only fair that Donald's widow gave of her labor. She would inherit Donald's half of the farm. Her lips tightening, she thought of that visit from Lawyer Tipton several years before. He had explained to her mother that her father was now legally dead. After deserting them almost thirty years before, he had reappeared at the farm intermittently for a few years. But for the past fifteen he had neither returned nor sent any sort of message. What was more, public notices published throughout the country had brought no response. Therefore Mrs. Fallon was now legally free to dispose of her person and her property in any way she chose.

He had drawn up a will for her that same day, and she had signed it with an X. Each of her children was to receive a half interest in the farm. Flora had felt sullen resentment. Donald was no longer on the farm. He was in a place called Connecticut where, according to his last letter, he planned to marry the daughter of a Congregational minister. True, he had always sent back a good part of his wages from America and had promised to keep on sending money. Still, Flora would go on being the one who argued with the sheep-shearing crews over their wages, and who cooked meals for them, and, when an unseasonable blizzard struck, went out shawled to the eyes and with a lantern in her cold-numbed hand looking for lambs that otherwise might freeze to death.

The will had been changed, of course. Now Donald's fifty percent share of the property was to go to "my daughter-in-law, Maryann Fallon, to be held in trust for my grandson, James Fallon."

Still more reason why Maryann should feel obliged to do all that she could to make the pig farm prosper. It was her son who would reap the benefit someday.

Flora closed her eyes. Cheated of some of her sleep, she would feel tired in the morning. And yet she knew that she

11

would wake as she always did—spring, summer, fall, winter—almost exactly fifteen minutes before daybreak. It was as if she had a clock inside her, mysteriously set to respond to the first faint light in the east, whether it appeared around three of a June morning or nine of a January one.

3

The narrow mattress that once had been Donald's was filled with cornhusks. He had never told her that. But she wondered if he had ever recalled this lumpy, crackling mattress when he lay on the wide featherbed that had been her parents' and grandparents'.

Don't think about Donald stretching out beside her in bed, then reaching over to wrap a curl of her hair around his finger—

Think about tomorrow.

Flora Fallon, in her reply to Maryann's letter, had made it plain that she would have to work. But at what? Was she to keep the house and prepare the meals, thus leaving Flora free to devote herself to the farm? That would be all right. She didn't mind housework. And it used to be that she had loved to cook—for Donald. She loved to see him standing tall and lean in the kitchen doorway. (Despite a hearty appetite, he had never put on fat.) He would sniff the air and say something like, "What are you cooking now? A feast of nectared sweets, like in that Shakespeare poem you read me?"

Often after supper she and Donald had read aloud to each other. Ever since their marriage he had been trying to fill in the gaps left by the sketchiest of childhood educations.

"Milton, Donald. Not Shakespeare. I haven't given a name to what I'm baking, but it's a fruit and nut pie."

Cooking was no longer a joy for her. Donald had taken with him her joy in so many small, everyday things—the fragrance of lavender-scented sheets in a cupboard, the odor of beeswax, the pattern of leaves cast by an afternoon sun on freshly starched curtains. Just the same, she would be able to keep house here, competently and uncomplainingly, both for the mother-in-law she liked and for the sister-in-law who rather frightened her.

If only it wasn't for the pig smell. It was in this room, not as overwhelming as outdoors, but still here.

Well, perhaps the cart driver was right. Perhaps she would get used to it in time.

But would she ever get used to life without Donald?

It rose before her then, that memory she usually tried to turn away from. But here in this darkened little room five thousand miles from home, lying on the cornhusk mattress that once had supported Donald's body, she let herself remember it.

That morning in early December the trees in their Connecticut farmyard had been coated with ice, making each twig a miniature prism that gave off rainbow colours. How she had loved the sight of ice-coated trees on a sunny morning! (Would she be able to take delight in it still, or was

14

that something else that Donald had taken with him? She didn't know. The rest of the Connecticut winter had been mild.)

The road that morning had been icy, too. Nevertheless, Donald was determined to attend an auction of wagons and wheel hoes and smaller farm implements in Keersville, five miles away. He had hitched his favorite mare, Nan, to the farmyard fence and then come back to the kitchen to drink another cup of hot tea against the cold journey ahead.

Taking down her red woolen shawl from its hook, she had wrapped it around her and then walked with him through the farmyard and its iridescent trees. A stray breeze, stirring the ice-encrusted twigs, made them give off a sound like chimes.

At the roadside he looked down at her, his blond hair hidden by a red woolen cap with earflaps, his eyes as blue as the winter sky. Then, smiling, he had lifted her by her elbows, kissed her mouth, and set her down. If any of their neighbors had been watching, he would have been scandalized. Yankees did not kiss their wives like that, not after six years of marriage, and not outdoors in broad daylight.

He had swung into the saddle and gently slapped Nan's reins against her to get her moving.

A fox, fiery red in the early sunlight, darted across Nan's path. Squealing, she reared. For a moment her rear hooves fought for purchase on the ice. Then she toppled backward, taking her rider with her.

Nan's four hooves pawed the empty air momentarily. Then she rolled over, scrambled awkwardly to her feet, and stood there trembling, icy breath streaming from her nostrils. Donald did not stir.

Somehow Maryann had already known, and yet the

knowledge lay on her lightly because she did not believe it. This could not have happened, not all in a moment, not to Donald. She knelt beside him.

Later the doctor said that his neck had been broken and that he had died instantly. Maryann knew that was not true. There had been time for him to realize that he was about to leave all that he had cherished. That knowledge was in the set stare—horrified, outraged—in the blue eyes that only moments before had looked down at her with merriment and love.

She turned over on the cornhusk mattress that had once borne Donald's body. She had not wept once during those weeks at sea. How could she, in a cabin shared with three other women? She had not wept on the clattering, coal-smelling train that had brought her from Liverpool to Leeds, nor in that jolting cart.

But now she let the sobs shake her whole body.

4

A sharp knocking. "Wake up! Time for breakfast."

Maryann opened her eyes and looked in puzzlement at the objects taking shape in the gray light. A ladderback chair. A rough stand holding a white pitcher and basin. Then she saw her portmanteau standing against the wall and knew where she was.

"All right!" she called. "I'm awake."

Last night she had used about half the cold water in the pitcher, trying to give herself as adequate a sponge bath as possible. True, the day before the *Western Star* had docked in Liverpool, steerage-class passengers had been given buckets of water and cakes of yellow soap with which to wash themselves and their clothing. But after the train journey from Liverpool behind the smoke-belching engine and then the long ride over dusty roads in the cart, she had felt almost as dirty as she had during the passage across the Atlantic. Now, with what water was left in the pitcher,

17

she washed her face, holding the cold water cupped against her eyes in an effort to wake herself completely.

When she emerged into the main room, she was wearing an old and much-darned brown muslin dress, one she had washed and hung up to dry aboard ship. Flora was kneeling beside the fire, using a flat paddle to turn cakes on a griddle. From beneath a skirt of gray linsey protruded her bare, sturdy ankles and equally bare, wide feet.

Maryann said, "You're cooking breakfast?"

Flora nodded. "And before this I milked the cow. We've got only one. I sold the others."

"But if you'd called me—I can milk a cow. And I'd thought the cooking and housework would be my duties."

"Housework! Housework gets done when there's nothing else to do." Her gaze swept Maryann's slight figure. "You're not going to wear that dress, are you?"

"Why—why, yes. I know it's very old, but I thought that for housework—"

"You'll be doing outdoor work."

She had worked outdoors on her and Donald's small farm. She had milked cows, fed chickens, harvested corn. Once when Donald had sprained his back badly, she had chopped wood for more than a week. Another time, when their plow horse developed glanders, she had held the plow handles while Donald, broad chest straining against a leather band, had drawn the broad blade through unbroken ground. And on many of those occasions she had worn this brown dress.

"I've worn this for farm work."

"Not for pig farming you haven't." Flora flipped a cake onto a pewter plate. "And take off those shoes and stockings."

18

Maryann said, bewildered, "You mean, work barefoot?"

"And barelegged. Feet and legs are easier to wash than stockings and shoes." As the girl looked at her dumbfounded, she went on. "Of course, in cold weather you can wear burlap foot and leg wrappings and leave them in the cow shed at night. Or boots, if you want to lay out the cost of them. But no need for either of those now. It'll seem a little cold at first, but you'll get used to it."

Used to it. Like getting used to the smell. Like getting used to the cold, hard shine of amusement in Flora's eyes. What, Maryann wondered, had made her sister-in-law the way she was? Whatever the reasons, Maryann could sense in the other woman a spitefulness, a cruelty, a willingness to take advantage of any vulnerability that others might display.

A creak of wheels outside and the thud of hooves on soft earth. Looking through a window's small panes, Maryann saw a corpulent man in a homespun shirt and worn leather breeches climb down from the driver's seat of a farm wagon. She said, "Who—"

"That's Toby Wells. He gathers swill from farms around here and brings it to me every morning."

Swill. Kitchen refuse. Again Maryann felt her stomach turn.

The man had lowered the wagon's tailgate and was placing wooden buckets on the ground. "I add sorghum and rye to the swill," Flora said, "before I feed it to them." As if the pigs knew that the wagon's arrival meant breakfast was near, loud squeals sounded from some pens near the house.

Flora poured tea from a pot on the hearth into a thick white mug, placed the mug beside the two flatcakes on the pewter plate. "You'll find forks in the table drawer over there and a wooden tray over there on the dresser. Take this to Ma, and then come back and eat your own breakfast."

Maryann carried the tray into her mother-in-law's room, placed it on her lap. The aging face framed by the ruffled cap, Maryann decided, did not in any way resemble her son's. It was only the smile and the expression in the gray-blue eyes that brought poignant reminders of Donald.

"Did you sleep well, Maryann?" It was not just a polite inquiry. Plainly, she had been concerned about her daughter-in-law's first night in this house.

"Yes, thank you." Once her crying was over, she had plunged into the deep, dreamless sleep of utter exhaustion. Undoubtedly, she would still be sleeping if Flora had not aroused her.

"Maryann?"

"Yes?"

The woman hesitated, then went on swiftly. "Don't let my daughter slavedrive you. She'll work you until you drop, if you let her."

Maryann murmured something noncommittal.

"It seems an awful thing for a woman to say about her own daughter, but I think she was born like that, cold and greedy, thinking she had a right to anything she could get." She paused, then essayed a small joke. "Maybe it was my calling her Flora. That means flower, you know."

"Yes, I know."

"You'd better get out and get your own breakfast, before she realizes we were probably talking about her. No, wait. I've got one question."

Maryann felt an inward shrinking. She didn't want to

talk about the moment Donald had left her, not this morning in this house, not even to the woman who must have
loved him so very much.

But Mrs. Fallon didn't ask her about her son's death.
Instead she said, "About my grandson. Does he favor you
or his father?"

She thought of her son's face, a face still too small and
too pale, although less so than early last summer, when
they had nearly lost him to typhoid. "It's too soon to be
sure, but I don't think he will resemble either of us very
much. If anything, I would say he looks like you."

It was true. Jaimie's eyes were bluish-gray like his grandmother's, and his nose gave promise of being slightly tilted
at the end like hers.

She gave a delighted smile. "I'm glad," she said; then
in a lower voice, "Remember what I said about Flora."

Less than half an hour later, Maryann stood beside Flora
on the bare earth in front of the house. Maryann had exchanged her brown muslin for a gray cotton skirt and blouse
that Flora had given her, both of them ragged but mercifully
clean. Like Flora, she wore neither shoes nor stockings.

The swill man, after placing more than a dozen buckets
in a row, had driven off. The sun was up now, but the air
was still chill on Maryann's feet and legs. As Flora had
instructed, she had tied a length of cloth around her legs
just below her hips and then bloused her skirts until they
barely reached her knees.

"Now, watch me so you can do it, too." From a large
burlap bag, Flora took three handfuls of rye and added
them to a nearly full bucket of swill. Next, she dipped a
tin cup into a barrel of molasses and added the cupful to

21

the swill. Finally, she stirred the mixture with a long wooden paddle. Fumes rose. Maryann's stomach churned. In a nearby pen, pigs squealed with rapturous anticipation.

"Now I'll load buckets into the handcart and wheel it to the pens farthest away. You take buckets over to that near pen. No, take two at once. Saves time and gives you better balance. But leave one bucket outside the pen until you've emptied the first one into the trough. Otherwise, they'll be upsetting a full bucket. Fill the trough gradually, so that they won't slop some of the swill onto the ground and waste it.

"And for heaven's sake, fasten the gate behind you before you do anything else. Otherwise, we'll be chasing pigs the rest of the morning."

Moments later, Maryann stood in the soft mud inside the locked pen, pouring the evil-smelling stuff slowly into the trough. Mud oozed between her toes, covered her feet to the ankles. Half-grown pigs, not squealing now but grunting, pressed against her legs as they struggled for places at the trough.

The sound of a horse's hooves somewhere behind her. Fighting nausea, she did not turn but kept on emptying the last of the swill in the bucket.

"Good morning, lass."

She turned then, the empty bucket in her hand. Outside the pen a stout man of sixty-odd sat on a handsome bay horse. Since no hair showed beneath his beaver hat, she judged him to be bald. The florid complexion of a brandy lover contrasted with his small blue eyes. His bottle-green jacket and fawn-colored breeches appeared to be of the very best woolen, and his highly polished brown riding boots glistened in the morning sunlight.

He asked, smiling, "What's your name, lass?"

She did not relish being called lass. "My name is Maryann Fallon, Mrs. Donald Fallon."

His smile wavered. "Oh, yes. I was sorry indeed to hear of Donald Fallon's death. Some kind of accident, wasn't it?"

She nodded.

"And so you've come to us clear from America."

That seemed to demand no reply, and so she made none.

"My name is Athaire, Sir Rodney Athaire."

Where had she heard that name? Oh, yes. From the cart driver yesterday. He had said that the beautiful house, pouring lamplight from its windows onto the lake's hovering mist, belonged to some people named Athaire.

"I often ride this way," he said. "My great-grandfather once owned all this land. It wasn't entailed, worse luck, so he was able to sell most of it to support his taste for gambling. But I like to have a look around now and then. And I wanted especially to see this place, now that Flora Fallon has given up sheep for pigs. Different kinds of enterprises interest me."

To judge by the way he was staring at her legs, female anatomy held even greater interest for him. She fought down the impulse to untie the cloth strip that held her skirts knee high. It would take more than the stare of a lecherous old man to cause her to let several inches of her hem soak in that mixture of mud, swill, and heaven knew what else.

She opened the gate, closed and latched it behind her, set down the empty bucket, and picked up the full one. "If you'll excuse me, Sir Rodney, I'd best get on with my work."

"Now, wait a minute, my girl. Listen to me."

"Yes?"

"Put down that damned bucket."

Her face expressionless, she set it down.

"A pig farm is no place for you."

She thought but didn't say, You are right about that.

"How would you like to come to us at Windmere? Not belowstairs. I can see that's not for you. But may I suggest assistant parlormaid? Perhaps in time you might even become my wife's personal maid. I gained the impression last week that she is dissatisfied with her present one. Can't sew buttons on properly, or something of the sort. Anyway, whatever your duties on the Windmere staff, they would be more pleasant than this."

She thought, All my duties? Including sharing your bed at night?

"Thank you, Sir Rodney, but I prefer to stay here. My husband was born on this farm. It was his home, and therefore it is now my home, too."

She turned, unlatched the gate, picked up the bucket. He said, amusement in his voice, "My offer will remain open. Perhaps in time you will change your mind about making this place your home."

Not replying, she went inside the pen, latched the gate, carried the bucket over to the trough. She heard the horse turn with a jingle of bridle and creak of leather. Then the hooves retreated. Pouring the noxious liquid into the trough, feeling the young pigs bump against her legs, she wondered if Sir Rodney was right. Would she, in a few weeks, feel that anything was better than staying here?

She looked to her left. About a hundred feet down the

sloping road, Sir Rodney had stopped to talk to Flora as she stood outside a pen, her hands grasping the handle of her cart. He rode on, and Flora began to push the cart up the slope.

She waited beside the young pigs' pen until Maryann emerged, the empty bucket in her hand. For the first time, Maryann saw a broad smile on her sister-in-law's lips. "What did he offer you?" Flora asked. "A shilling to meet him in the nearest barn loft?"

"He asked me to join the staff at his house. Assistant parlormaid, or something of the sort."

Flora laughed, showing teeth so square and strong-looking that Maryann was reminded inevitably of a horse. "I hope you said no."

"Of course I did!"

"If you stay here and work hard and if we have the right luck, we can be rich in five years, or maybe ten. There you'd be lucky to earn a few pounds a year. And besides, you'd have to put up with Sir Rodney.

"Not that he'd be likely to put you in the family way," she went on, again with that broad smile. "He's past all that, I hear. A slap and tickle, that's all he can manage. Still, I imagine not even that would set well with you."

Her smile vanished. "All right," she said. "Now we'll do more of the pens lower down. Help me load up the cart."

5

By nine that night, Maryann was again stretched out on the cornhusk mattress. Her body inside the flannel nightdress was as clean as she could make it. Before supper she had stood beside the outdoor pump, hitched her skirts even higher, and washed the mud from her legs. Then she had rubbed them with the cake of yellow soap she had brought off the ship with her. In her own room she had stripped off Flora's skirt and blouse and her own underclothing, taken a sponge bath, and then donned the old brown muslin she had worn first that morning.

She was clean. Yet she had a sense that the smell still clung to her. And she was tired, more than she should be. True, she had worked hard that day. But in the past she had sometimes worked even harder, especially when she and Donald were getting that rundown farm outside Fernshaw, Connecticut, back into shape.

She thought of what Fernshaw was like on spring nights

like this one. The village square with its statue of Admiral Abraham Fernshaw, a local hero who had died in the War of 1812. Her father's white-steepled Congregational church fronting the square along with the a score of handsome frame houses, most of them built before the Revolution. Already the willow trees would be in leaf, trailing their branches along the red-brick sidewalk. The air would be perfumed with narcissus blooming in dooryards and with the scent of green growing things in the farms outside the village.

Until now, Maryann had never been more than twenty miles away from Fernshaw. She had grown up in the parsonage, a happier child than most. True, her mother's death when Maryann was eight had been a bewildering blow. But when she recovered from it, she had felt even closer to her father. She adored everything about him. His long-fingered, sensitive hands. His very thin, high-cheekboned face. Most of all, she had loved his heart, which was kind without being sentimental, and his mind, which could be realistic without being cold.

She had gone through the village school and then to the Brewster Young Ladies Academy, eight miles away. Its course of study was "advanced," even shockingly so. It offered not just classes in French, deportment, domestic management, and china painting but also in Greek, Latin, and biology. The Academy was not cheap. If her father had not owned a tenant farm near Fernshaw, he would not have been able to send her there. She had been glad of the chance to attend the Academy. Even so, she felt that it was in her father's library that she had gained most of her education. He had locked away his Rabelais, *Kama Sutra*, and a few other works. But she had been free to read anything remaining on the shelves, even Gibbon with his ribald footnotes.

After her graduation from the Academy, she had spent three years as her father's housekeeper and hostess. By that time she was twenty-one, old for a maiden in Fernshaw.

She had had suitors. There had been the banker's son, a young man who, perhaps because of the fear inspired in him since early childhood by an overbearing father, had damp hands and a giggle. There had been Adam Searle, who with his father ran the general store, and who at the age of thirty-two was already a widower with five-year-old twin girls to raise. There were also young farmers and craftsmen who had eyed her covertly but could not summon up the courage to approach the parson's daughter.

Maryann had realized that confirmed spinsterhood was only a few years ahead. Yet she was so happy with her life of presiding at her father's table, reading his books, visiting the sick on his behalf, and gathering with Fernshaw's young people at picnics and around the parsonage piano that she had found it hard to worry about the future.

Then one June morning she and her father had driven in his buggy to the blacksmith's shop in an alley off the square. The smith, John Apperson, had greeted the Reverend Lloyd with respectful cordiality.

Maryann's father had said, "I wonder if you could visit my tenant farm and see if the plow horses there need your attention. The Pelhams have been good tenants for many years, but they've grown old and a little forgetful."

"I sure will, Reverend. Either that, or I'll send my helper. He's really a farm lad, but believe me, Reverend, in one week he's caught on so you'd think he'd been blacksmithing for years." He had raised his voice. "Donald!"

A man in homsespun breeches and an undervest that left his arms bare to the shoulders had emerged from the blacksmith's shed, a heavy hammer still in his hand. He had been sweating, and the undervest was plastered to him so that the contours of his muscled chest showed. He was a young giant, at least six foot three. His hair, blond and curly, gleamed in the sunlight. His eyes were the bluest Maryann had ever seen.

Her heart seemed to turn over in her chest. Reading that phrase in books, she had felt a little scornful of it. How could one's heart seem to turn over? Now she knew.

John Apperson said, "Reverend, this is Donald Fallon, just two weeks off the boat from England. Donald, this is the Reverend Lloyd."

His remarkable smile lit up Donald Fallon's face. He transferred the hammer to his left hand, wiped his right palm on his breeches leg, and then took the hand James Lloyd had extended.

"And this is the reverend's daughter, Miss Lloyd."

His smile changed as he looked at her, became almost grave. His broad, bare shoulders made a slight bow, unstudied but graceful.

Maryann was unusually quiet as they started home. Then, suddenly sure that her father had noticed her silence, she began to talk about the first thing that came into her head. But the look on her father's face—thoughtful, somewhat dismayed, but also rather amused—did not alter.

Donald Fallon, in a brown coat and trousers that were obviously store-bought and obviously new, came to church the following Sunday morning. Even though he sat well to her left and several rows behind her, she could feel his gaze on her profile. He was there again the next Sunday, and the next.

Maryann began to sleep badly and to forget just what orders she had given to Matty, the maid-of-all-work.

On the last Sunday in July, Maryann stood beside her father after the service, shaking hands with the congregation. Donald took her hand in his big warm one, and then her father's.

The reverend said, "Will you come to our house for one o'clock dinner, Donald?"

His words came to Maryann as a complete surprise. But even though Donald's fair skin reddened with pleasure, Maryann had the feeling that he was not surprised, not entirely.

"That I will, Reverend. And thank you very much."

When the last of the congregation had left, Maryann and Reverend Lloyd walked around the corner of the church to the parsonage. In the entrance hall Maryann said, almost sternly, "Father, I want to speak to you."

"There is some sort of mixup here. That sounds like something I should say to you."

In his book-lined study she faced him. "You've been seeing Donald Fallon, haven't you?"

"Stranger and stranger. That certainly sounds like a speech I should be making to you."

"Haven't you?"

"Yes. We had a long talk last week when I took Benny in to be shod, and another yesterday."

"Why? What did you talk about?"

"Surely you know the answer to that." The faintest uncertainty came into his voice. "Or could I be wrong? Are you or aren't you ready to accept Donald Fallon as a suitor?"

Maryann felt color in her cheeks. "Yes."

"In fact, you're head over heels in love with him, aren't you?"

"Yes." Then she burst out, "But I thought I must never let you know that." In a community where almost half the people could do nothing more than sign their own names, James Lloyd spoke not only the classical languages but French and German, too. How could he accept a blacksmith as a son-in-law?

Her father said, "Donald's not stupid, you know."

"Oh, I know," she said fervently. She knew it instinctively, even though they had exchanged only a few dozen words. "But still, a blacksmith—"

"That should not be the most important consideration. Besides, he has been a blacksmith for only a few weeks. Before that he was a farmer, and he can be again. The Fallons raise sheep, but also some corn—maize, he calls it—and other crops."

"But farms cost money!"

"That is what Donald and I were discussing yesterday. Our tenants are about to leave the farm. They think they'll be better off living with their son's family. You and Donald could take over the farm." He smiled. "That is, of course, if after a courtship of suitable duration you decided to accept Donald."

He pulled out his thick gold watch and snapped its case open. "Almost one. Shouldn't you see how Matty is getting along with dinner?"

31

Their courtship was brief indeed. Two weeks later as they took an evening walk around the village square, he asked her to marry him, and she promptly accepted. Their engagement was unorthodox, too. During the late afternoons and the long summer twilight after the smithy had closed, they worked on the farm, carrying to the town dump whole cartloads of junk that the elderly tenants had accumulated, replacing weak floorboards, and repairing the roof, with Maryann climbing halfway up the ladder to hand her beloved bundles of shingles and boxes of nails.

The farm would remain in his name, Maryann's father explained to them. That was because the farm was mortgaged on very favorable terms, which the bank would not extend to a new mortgage-holder. But of course at his death, by which time the mortgage would have been long since paid, the property would be theirs. In the meantime, his wedding present to them would be new farm implements and two milch cows.

While they worked on the house they expected to live in for the rest of their lives, Donald talked of that other farm back in Yorkshire. She already knew that he had been sending part of his smithy wages home to his invalid mother and to his sister. Scrupulously, he had told her that even before he proposed to her.

"And Maryann, I'll feel I have to keep sending what money I can even after we are married. I promised Flora that."

"Then you must keep your promise."

They were married one afternoon in early September. In a buggy to which someone had affixed white satin bows and a "Just Married" sign, they drove five miles to the farm, past fields of ripened corn.

Maryann felt happy and yet nervous. There was this wedding night matter ahead. Not that her father had talked to her about it. "I like to think of myself as advanced," he said, "especially for a man of the cloth, but I am not *that* advanced. There are some matters about which you must turn to someone else. I suggest Grace Whitterby."

Mrs. Whitterby, a widow of about Reverend Lloyd's age, was his lifelong friend. When Maryann went to see her, Mrs. Whitterby was both vague and unreassuring. "The first time may be quite painful, and even after that you probably won't like it. Just keep in mind that it is the price a woman must pay if she wants children and the support and protection of a husband."

A few hours later, in the big double bed, Maryann found out just how wrong Mrs. Whitterby had been. Maryann did not find it all that painful. And in the days and nights that followed, she came to bring to their lovemaking an ardor that seemed to shock Donald even as it delighted him. Arms braced on either side of her body, broad chest shiny with sweat, he would look down at her and laugh. "Lass, lass! And you a parson's daughter."

Because of all that lovemaking, Maryann had thought that they would probably celebrate parenthood before their first anniversary. They did not. Two years passed, two and a half. Then, with their third anniversary only weeks away, she finally knew that she was pregnant.

Before they were married, Donald had suggested that they read aloud to each other, so that he might make up for his sketchy education. As newlyweds, they had found more exciting uses for their leisure hours than reading. Even after their first ardor had waned, they found many tasks—renewing the treads on the staircase, blacking the fireplace andirons—to occupy the time between supper and going to bed.

But after she became pregnant, everything was different. For one thing, she performed no heavy work, indoors or out. As placid as their cow Dulcie, who was also about to reproduce, she moved about her household tasks. In the evenings she and Donald read aloud to each other from *Romeo and Juliet*, and *David Copperfield*, and the recently published *House of Seven Gables*. Even though she herself read smoothly and Donald often stumbled over words, Maryann realized that their reading enriched him as much or even more than it did her. Once he said, "This Shakespeare. He says something like 'the uncertain glory of an April day.' You think of other ways to say it, like a sunny April day that may turn cloudy later on. But that's not as good as what he said. Is that genius, being able to say things the best way possible?"

"Maybe so."

Their son was born on an April day not of uncertain glory, but of drenching rain. The rain did nothing to lessen her exultance when the midwife laid the child in her arms.

Sitting beside the bed, Donald touched a fingertip to the small head with its fuzz of pale hair. "What shall we call him?"

"Donald, of course."

Her husband shook his head. "He should be James, after your father. We owe him everything—the farm, the baby, each other. What I mean is, if he hadn't encouraged me, I would never have come near you. I wouldn't have had the courage."

"All right. He will be James."

34

Jaimie was almost three years old that day when the horse reared on the icy road and toppled backward, leaving Donald to stare at the sky with sightless eyes filled with horror and outrage.

6

In his bedroom at Windmere, with its twelve-foot-high ceilings and dark red velvet window draperies, Sir Rodney sat in a high-backed armchair after dinner and stared discontentedly at the flames leaping in the fireplace. Why couldn't he get that American girl at the Fallon farm out of his mind? Why did he keep seeing her as she stood there, bare legs smeared with mud, eyes haughty in her thin face?

She really wasn't the sort that usually attracted him. Not young enough, for one thing. He'd judged her to be in her middle twenties. And she was so thin. He liked to be able to get a real handful of breast or buttock, especially since —alas!—that was the only way he could enjoy a woman nowadays.

He wondered just how many people knew that he had been impotent for the past several years. His wife Elaine? Probably, although it might be that she assumed he had come to prefer other companionship, just as she preferred Jonathan Burke.

The thought of Jonathan—superlatively handsome Jonathan—made him frown with displeasure that held only a touch of jealously. Jonathan was supposed to be steward here at Windmere. That was what Sir Rodney had hired him for, at Lady Athaire's insistence. But how did he spend his time? Playing cards with Elaine, reading with Elaine, reading poetry to her and to a gathering of her friends in her sitting room.

And the worst part was that Sir Rodney could do nothing about it. Often his father-in-law had loaned him money, money that both men knew would not be repaid. One word from Elaine, and there would be no more such loans.

His thoughts returned to the American girl. How could she possibly prefer a pig farm to Windmere? Surely she must have realized that he was offering her more than a position as a servant. He would have been willing to give her money and costly trinkets. Even if his interest in her lasted only a few months, she would return to the Fallon farm considerably richer than when she came here.

He got up and began to pace the thick Turkish carpet. Perhaps because of his annoyance over the girl, an impulse had come to him, one he wanted to resist.

But why resist? It had been months since he had visited that room at the end of the corridor. And afterward he always felt better, more at peace with himself.

He went to the picture beside the massive oak door. The oil landscape was so dim with age that it was hard to make out that it was a hunting scene with a pack of hounds surrounding a stag. He took down the picture, revealing the dials of a steel safe, and leaned the picture against the wall. He turned the dials, opened the door. Only one object lay on the safe's floor—a large iron key. He restored the picture to its place, closed the safe door, and stepped out into the candlelit corridor. Five years earlier he had installed gas jets in Windmere's rooms, but the lustrously paneled halls were still lighted by traditional—and more expensive— wax tapers set in wall brackets.

Across the hall, Martin Cramer was opening the door of his own room. Hand on the knob, he turned and said, "Good evening, Sir Rodney."

"Evening."

Sir Rodney did not like Martin Cramer. It was nothing you could put your finger on. The fellow always seemed respectful enough, as befitted a farmer's son addressing a fourth baronet. And certainly he was useful. Even though handsome young Jonathan was the titular steward, it was this tall, quiet thirty-five-year-old who actually managed Windmere and what remained of its tenant farms. But there was something about him—a too-independent set to his shoulders, an almost sardonic gleam in his dark eyes—that rubbed Sir Rodney the wrong way.

He turned and went down the hall. Martin looked after him for a moment. What did the old boy keep in that always-locked room? An extensive collection of pornographic literature and art? Probably.

Martin felt contempt for the whole crew at Windmere. Sir Rodney, snuggling in linen closets with giggly housemaids, passing his days in idleness, showing little concern for the welfare of his tenants or the productivity of their farms. Lady Elaine, whom Martin had seen eyeing with interest even a new stableboy leading her favorite mount from its stall. Young Rodney, the fifteen-year-old son and heir, who had been sent down from Eton for cheating on his Greek examinations and from Winchester for card gambling and who was now traveling through Europe with a tutor.

And then there was Jonathan Burke. The tolerant contempt he felt for Jonathan had turned, after more than a year here at Windmere, into abhorrence. Gradually Martin had realized that there was no depravity the younger man might not perform, and not just to bring some benefit to himself. Sometimes he seemed to act out of sheer love of evil.

Martin went into his room. Even though it was probably the plainest of the Windmere rooms set aside for family and guests, it was still far more luxurious than anything he had known during his growing-up years or his three years as an Oxford don. Martin was more than content with it and with his whole situation, including his bargain with Jonathan. Jonathan collected a steward's salary, devoted himself to Lady Elaine, and gave half that salary to Martin, who actually managed the estate. By Spartan living, Martin had been able to save most of the money Jonathan turned over to him. What was more, he was gaining the experience he needed to help him bring his dream to reality, a dream that encompassed a strange new country and herds of cattle moving across vast spaces.

Enough light came from the corridor to guide him across the room to his desk and the gas jet above it. He lit the gas, pulled out his chair. Opening the account book that contained the records of the remaining Windmere farms, he set to work.

Down the hall, Sir Rodney unlocked a door, swung it back. He lit the nearest gas jet, closed the door, and then went about the room, lighting more jets and even a five-branched candelabra that stood on the fireplace mantel. On these occasions he liked to have the room brilliantly lit, as if for a ball.

With a smaller key, one of several on a ring he took from his breeches pocket, he unlocked the mirrored doors of an armoire, swung them wide. There they hung in all their glory—gowns of ruby-red velvet, ice-blue brocade, yellow satin, gowns in almost every color of the rainbow.

The ice-blue gown was new. A Parisian of his acquaintance, a man who shared his proclivities, had brought the gown and shipped it to a room Sir Rodney maintained in an inn just outside of London. A week ago he had unpacked the dress and admired it but had felt no impulse to try it on. Instead, he had packed it in his valise, brought it to Windmere, and locked it away in the armoire against the time he would feel a desire to wear it.

Sir Rodney had no idea whence those impulses came nor what they meant. Certainly it didn't mean he was a lover of men. That sort of thing had never interested him, not even at preparatory school or at Oxford, where not a few of his classmates had experimented with what some called "Greek love."

Nor did he feel that it meant that in some corner of his being he wanted to be a woman. God! Who would want to be a woman? Empty-headed, educated poorly or not at all, cursed with the inconvenience of childbearing, and—unless, like Elaine, she had a rich father—weilding little or no power in her own household, let alone in the world outside.

No, he didn't want to be a woman. And yet several times

each year he felt a need to prove to himself that he could *look* like a woman, and a handsome one at that.

With another of the small keys he opened a chest. Inhaling the pleasant scent of cedar, he took out a corselet —not the ordinary sort, but one that reached higher on the body. Pads had been sewn inside it, giving the wearer the appearance of having womanly breasts. He laid the corselet on a chair. Deeper in the chest were ruffled pantalets, silk stockings, garters.

He stripped, then began to dress leisurely, choosing pantalets and stockings with care. From a cloth bag at the bottom of the chest he took out silver brocade slippers.

Back at the armoire he shoved dresses aside to reveal a set of hoops on their stand in one corner. The hoops had also been sent to him some time ago, when they first became fashionable. He tied the tape fasteners around his waist, delighting in the way the hoops tilted and swayed around his pantaletted legs. Then the dress. He slid it over his head and down over the hoops, then did up the little brocaded buttons that reached from the waist to the neckline.

All the time he dressed, he had avoided looking into any of the room's many mirrors. He still avoided doing so. He knew that, no matter how magnificent he looked from the neck down, his bald head would make him a figure of fun.

How he hated his baldness! How he wished he had lived a hundred years ago, when gentlemen, no matter what their age or the condition of their own hair, had worn perukes!

He went to a tall, narrow cabinet in one corner, unlocked it. Wigs stood on their faceless stands, each on its own shelf. Should it be the glowing titian? The black one, shiny as sable? The pale yellow? Yellow, he decided. It would be best with the ice-blue brocade.

He fitted the wig, with its smooth crown and its cluster of curls at the nape of the neck, onto his head. Only then did he close the mirrored doors of the armoire and look at his image.

He caught his breath. How wonderful he looked already, even without paint or jewels! Moving more rapidly now, he went to a dressing table, unlocked its drawer, took out a jewelry box, a rouge pot. With his fingers he delicately colored his cheeks and lips. He put on a many-stranded pearl necklace. Real pearls that had been in the family since before the first baronetcy had been granted. Elaine, who disliked pearls—they made the complexion look dull, she had said—apparently didn't even know they were missing from the small vault in her boudoir. When she and Rodney were first married, she had looked at the pearls, closed the lid of their black velvet box, and apparently never thought of them again.

Now he walked back to the armoire and again looked at his full-length reflection. *Magnifique!* The wide hoopskirt made his waist look almost slender by contrast. The ice-blue color of the gown, as well as the painted flush high on his cheekbones, made his eyes look bright. He opened one door of the armoire long enough to take down from its shelf an ostrich-feather fan of darker blue. He spread the fan wide and held it against his bosom.

He imagined himself descending the stairs of one of the great houses of London, with the gazes of all the other ballgoers fastened upon him.

But alas, that could never be. No one but his Parisian

friend and three other men of similar inclination must ever know. If he were caught in outright buggery, he might be able to live it down. If he were caught cheating at cards, he might live that down, too. But if someone saw him as he looked now and spread the story, ridicule would follow him the rest of his days.

For a few minutes more, he contemplated his image. Then, feeling calmer and somehow even stronger than when he had come into this room, he began to divest himself of the feminine finery and change back into his ordinary garb.

7

Maryann had not become used to the smell, not even after three weeks.

Those weeks had not been entirely unpleasant. After the last of the chores, after she had bathed and eaten supper, Maryann would sit by Mrs. Fallon's bed for a while. By tacit agreement, they seldom even mentioned their present circumstances. Instead they talked of the man who had been the older woman's son and the younger one's husband and of the little boy who, God willing, would grow up with them here in England.

As the days lengthened toward summer, Maryann sometimes sacrificed an hour or so of precious sleep by walking down the lane between the pens in the evening, crossing the road, and climbing a low stone wall. Then she would be in a neighbor's field—Gilchrist, Flora had said their name was—among the long grasses and the about-to-blossom daisies and the grazing sheep. They would regard her with

blank, incurious eyes, move away a little, and resume nib-
bling the grass. She would sit with her legs curled around
her under her skirt and think of home.

She always tried to think of her peaceful growing-up
years in the parsonage or, later on, those often ecstatically
happy years with Donald. But inevitably, more recent
memories would sometimes engulf her.

After Donald's death, there had been no question of her
trying to run the farm alone, with its horses and cows and
chickens to feed and, later on, its fields to till and plant.
Parishioners of her father's, farmers named Yerxa who lived
about a mile from Donald and Maryann's place, came to
the rescue. With five grown and half-grown sons and three
daughters, one in her early twenties and two still in knee-
length dresses, the Yerxas would well be able to handle
the situation for a few months. Maryann and Jaimie moved
into town to the parsonage.

She had thought that life had done its worst to her and
that now she would live out her years in quiet grief. In
mid-January she had learned how wrong she was. Typhoid
had struck Fernshaw and the neighboring towns. Now as
thin as a shadow, Maryann did not catch the disease. Lively
young James and his seemingly robust grandfather did.
Feeling that the whole world had turned into a nightmare,
Maryann had moved between the two beds. While Matty
took over, she would sleep for a few hours. Then she would
go back to bathing fevered faces and bodies, spooning medicine into the infant mouth and the aging one.

During a late afternoon visit, stout Dr. Corwith, who
had presided at her own birth, told her that her son would
recover.

45

While she stood there, feeling almost faint with relief, he added gently, "But I think you should prepare yourself to lose your father."

After a stunned moment she cried, "But he's not really old! He's still in his fifties."

"I know. But about a year ago he developed a heart condition. He didn't want to worry you with it. Now, don't look like that, Maryann. I didn't say he will leave us. I'm just saying we must face the probability."

The next night, as she bent over him, her father's hand—so fevered that she could feel its heat through her sleeve—caught her arm so that she bent even closer.

"The farm," he whispered, His lips were cracked, his breath fetid. "I'm sorry, darling. You won't have the farm."

Delirious, she thought. Gently freeing her arm, she poured medicine into a spoon. He died a little after three that morning, while she lay in exhausted slumber.

It wasn't until her lawyer talked to her a week later that she learned what her father had meant. True, he had left the farm to her, but it hadn't been his to leave. The bank owned it.

Confident that he had many years ahead of him, her father had taken out a second mortgage on the farm to pay for his "wedding gift" of farm equipment and livestock. To help himself meet the mortgage payments, he had begun to invest in stocks issued by the All New England Railroad Company.

The line had failed. James Lloyd had begun to default on his mortgage payments.

The bank had been the farm's real owner since a few days before Donald's death. The bank president had acceded to the Reverend's plea that Maryann not be told until she had recovered from her first raw grief. But now there was no help for it. She had to know.

But she need not move from the parsonage right away. The church would engage a new pastor, of course, but its elders had decided that for a while he could board with a parishioner.

When the lawyer had gone, Maryann in her black dress sat motionless in a square of February sunlight that fell through the window onto her rocking chair. Against the wall opposite, Jaimie lay asleep in his crib, his small face still pale from the sickness that had almost killed him. Maryann forced herself to face the fact that she and her son were penniless, or almost. What did they have? Perhaps the bank would not claim the furniture, most of it made by Donald, at the farm. Here in the parsonage there was some furniture that had belonged to her father rather than the church. There were his books, and his gold watch, and her ruby brooch that had been her mother's. How much would all that bring? At most, barely enough to support herself and her child for a few months. And after that they would have nothing.

No, wait. Donald's mother owned a farm in Yorkshire, England. It would be left, Donald had told her, to his older sister and himself. But surely Donald's inheritance had become Jaimie's now.

Rising, she took from a metal trunk the box of mementoes she had brought from the farm. Soon she found the reply his sister had sent to Donald's letter telling of his marriage. The letter, misspelled and mispunctuated and cold in tone, had said she hoped her brother had done the "rite" thing and then proceeded to a brief mention of their mother's continued invalidism and the falling prices for wool. Having read it nearly five years ago, Maryann did not read it again but merely noted the return address on the envelope: Flora Fallon, Fallon Farm, near Elmsford, Yorkshire.

Maryann dispatched a letter. While she waited anxiously for the reply, she turned what few assets she had into cash. It amounted to less than she had hoped for, but at least it should cover third-class passage for Jaimie and herself.

The daffodils beside the parsonage porch were already in bud when Flora Fallon's reply arrived.

"Cum if you like. Lord knows I cud use your help. But don't bring your boy. This farm is no place for a sikly child. He can cum later, or you can go back and fetch him.

(No mention of the fact that the Fallon farm no longer raised sheep, only pigs. Why, Maryann wondered later? Had Flora been really eager for someone to help out, too eager to risk causing Maryann to change her mind?)

As cold and curt as the letter was, Maryann realized it made sense. Oh, her little son was no longer "sikly." But he was still definitely frail. Maryann herself had quailed at the thought of taking such a young child on a sea voyage. Almost certainly the cabin would be crowded, and the food might be unwholesome.

Perhaps better to follow Flora Fallon's advice. She might not be as unfriendly as she sounded, only short-spoken, like many country people. In time, she and Flora could become friends. In time, Jaimie's aunt and grandmother might be almost as eager for the little boy's presence as she herself would be.

But where could Jaimie stay until then?

48

The next day the church sexton drove her and Jaimie out to the Yerxa farm in his buggy. In the crowded kitchen Maryann sat with Jaimie on her lap.

Her round face beaming, Mrs. Yerxa said that she would not only take care of Jaimie for as long as necessary but would enjoy it. "It will be nice to have a baby in the house again."

Maryann looked at the Yerxa daughter pumping water into the tin sink. Another daughter stood on a high stool taking a jar down from a shelf. A boy of about twelve was stacking firewood beside the wide fireplace. "You're sure? There are already so many of you."

"That's why one more won't be any trouble."

"As soon as I can, I'll send money for his keep."

"Now, how much could a little fella like that eat? If you feel you have to send money, do so, but we won't mind if you don't. And as for him getting over to you, our Clara has her heart set on a trip to England." The eldest of the Yerxa offspring, Clara taught in the village school. "No reason why she shouldn't bring him to you when the time comes."

The next day, leaving her son in a neighbor's care, Maryann took the stage to New London. At the Star Line office she learned that early the following week a passenger ship would leave for Liverpool. Trying not to think of what it would be like to see water widening between herself and her little boy, she booked third-class passage. At the post office she wrote Flora Fallon, giving the approximate day of her arrival, and sent the letter by clipper ship.

On a sunny morning in late March the sexton again drove her and Jaimie to the Yerxa farm and waited outside. In

49

the crowded kitchen, small James went willingly into Mrs. Yerxa's arms and gave her his wide, untoothed smile. But when he gathered that his mother was going away without him, a terrible anguish came over his face. Struggling in Mrs. Yerxa's grasp, he held out his arms to Maryann.

"Mama has to do this," she said desperately. "Mama will be back for you. Now try to be a good boy, my darling."

He still wailed, still stretched out his arms. Feeling as if her heart literally bled, Maryann bolted out the door. When she reached the buggy she leaned against it, fighting down nausea.

The sexton extended a hand to help her up. When she sat beside him, she said, "Drive away fast."

On these evenings, a trespasser seated in a sheep-dotted meadow, Maryann would realize that the long twilight had faded. It must be well past nine, and she had to be up by four. She would maneuver her long skirts over the stone wall, cross the road, and then turn up the narrower one leading between the pens to the Fallon farmhouse.

8

The morning after the last of her trespasses into that sheep meadow, Maryann stood waiting for the swill man. It was her turn to mix the pig food. For some reason, she hated that chore most of all, even more than filling the troughs with the pigs jostling against her bare legs.

Toby Welch, the swill man, drove up. He opened the tailgate, took out the swill buckets, and set them down by the sack of barley and bucket of molasses she had brought down from the loft.

"My pay's due," he said. "A ha'penny a day for—let's see. May has thirty-one days—" He took a pencil stub and a dirty piece of paper from his breeches pocket.

Maryann said, "It comes to one shilling, thripence, ha'penny." It was from hearing Donald read Dickens aloud that she had learned how to say *thripence*.

Toby gave her a surprised stare and then began to write slowly, laboriously. At last he said, "That is right, lass."

"I'll get the money from my sister-in-law." Flora kept in a locked wooden box the shilling and pence needed to pay the swill man and occasionally a tinker or roof thatcher.

When Maryann emerged from the house, Toby said, "With a head for figures like that, it is too bad you are a lass."

Not answering, Maryann laid the coins on his outstretched palm.

"Up't the mine, they are looking for a paymaster-clerk."

She knew what mine he meant—the coal mine on the other side of the ridge beyond the Fallon land. Maryann had never seen the mine, but her mother-in-law had told her about it. Donald once had thought of going into the mine, before he and his sister and mother had decided that he would have a better chance of helping himself and his family if he went to America.

"Yes, too bad," Tony repeated. "Paymaster's wages is ten shillings a week."

Ten shillings! It was a fortune. If she had had that sort of wage, she would soon have enough not only to have her little son brought to England but to lodge the two of them somewhere away from this farm.

"A head for figures is almost wasted on a lass," Toby said. "The mine would never hire a woman. Paymastering is a man's job."

Yes, Maryann thought, some women had always done backbreaking work in fields and houses. But sitting at a desk while you added up figures, that was a man's job.

As Toby drove away, she added barley to one of the buckets and began to stir the mixture with the wooden paddle.

It was two days later, in the farthest pen from the house,

that she fell. She had just emptied the second of two buckets into the trough and had turned toward the gate when the piglet ran across her path. Trying to avoid the little animal, she slipped and pitched forward to the ground.

Cheek pressed into the mud, she lay still for a few seconds, less because the breath had been knocked out of her than because she felt overwhelmed by a sudden sense of outrage.

If there was any way to escape this life for something better, she would find it.

She got up and with the back of her hand wiped the mud from her face as best she could. Careful to latch the gate behind her, she carried the empty bucket to the handcart. By the time she pushed the cart to the top of the slope, she knew what she was going to do.

When she emerged from her room the next morning, she was wearing the brown cotton dress she had put on her first day in this house.

Flora stared at her. "Just where do you think you're going, all dressed up?"

"To the mine."

"The *mine*."

"Toby said a paymaster is needed there. I'm going to see if they will hire me."

"Hire you! Maryann, are you daft? Don't you know what *master* means? It means man. Whoever heard of a pay-*mistress*?"

"Nevertheless, I'm going to apply. If they need someone very badly, they may hire me."

Flora shrugged. "Go on, then. I guess I can spare you for a few hours, if it gets this foolishness out of your system."

Trying not to let her sister-in-law's words affect her,

Maryann ate a heartier than usual breakfast of oat cakes and sausage. She was going to need her strength. It was more than three miles to the mine, much of the way uphill.

As it turned out, she had to walk only part of the way. Soon after she turned off onto the main road, a farmer and his young son gave her a ride in their wagon. When she asked to be let off at the "side road leading up to the mine," the farmer looked at her curiously but made no comment.

The wagon deposited her at the foot of a road rising steeply between sheep meadows dotted with oak trees. She toiled upward, clutching the paper-wrapped parcel of bread and cheese that, in the unlikely but fervently hoped-for event of her being put to work on the spot, would become her mid-day meal. Nervous as she was, she still enjoyed the beauty of the June morning—the spilling of lark song from a cloudless sky, the daisies beginning to unfurl their white petals in the tall meadow grass, the occasional patch of blossoming hawthorn along the stone walls. Then she topped the crest of the hill, and the world was no longer so beautiful.

The mine, a gaping wound in the hillside, was about a hundred yards below her and a hundred feet to her right. A broad ledge in front of it, once no doubt grassy but now worn to bare earth, held a few rusting ore cars and a wooden building that, she was sure, housed the mine office.

Her heart beating fast, she descended the slope and turned to her right along the ledge. Even though it was not much past seven o'clock, all the miners must have been below, because when she looked into the mine entrance, all she saw were two tethered mules and a man with an oddly twisted body who leaned against a windlass. His pock-marked face looked at her with surprise.

She stopped in the open doorway of the wooden building.

A man seated at a wildly cluttered desk looked up at her with that same surprise.

"What do you—" He had been about to address her as "lass," but something in the poise of her small dark head and the erectness of her body in the old brown dress made him amend it to, "What do you want, miss?"

"I heard you were in need of a paymaster-clerk."

"American, aren't you?"

She nodded.

"Well, you heard right. I need a paymaster-clerk in the worst way, especially since tomorrow is Saturday."

"Payday, you mean?"

"Right. You know somebody who could fill the job? Husband? A brother, maybe?"

"No. Myself."

"You!" He looked astounded, then amused, then thoughtful. Finally he said, "Miner makes one shilling, sixpence a day. How much does he make in a week?"

"Nine shillings."

"That one was too easy."

He got to his feet, a tall sandy-haired man of about fifty, thin except for a bulging midriff. "Here. You'll need paper and pencil for this. Now this same miner loses one day's pay for not coming to work at all, two quarters of a day for being late, a day's pay for breaking his pickax—" He went on with the saga of the inept miner, who doubtless before the week was out would have lost his job.

"Now, how much did he make that week?"

Wielding the pencil, Maryann multiplied, substracted, and gave the answer. "Sixpence."

The man nodded. "What's your name?"

"Mrs. Fallon. Maryann Fallon."

"Well, mine's Clarence Clegg, and I'm the superintendent here. How is your handwriting?"

"Rather good, I think."

"On that same piece of paper write, 'In reply to your letter regarding the last visit of the inspector of mines—' That should be enough."

She wrote, handed him the paper. Again he nodded. "There's never been a woman in this job, but lord knows I have to have somebody, or I'll be out of a job myself. We'll pay you eight shillings a week."

"I heard a paymaster gets ten!"

"That's for a pay *master*, a man who has a family to support, or at least probably will have soon."

She thought of Jaimie, wailing with terror and reproach as he stretched out his arms to her. "Didn't it occur to you that I might have someone dependent upon me?" she wanted to say. But she must not, lest he withdraw his offer. And anyway, she could still save some money, even out of eight shillings. "Very well."

"Report tomorrow. Eight o'clock will be fine."

"Very well," she said again. Then: "What does that man standing just inside the mine do?"

"Him? He's the windlass man. Not fit for anything else, not since he was caught in a cave-in six years ago. He and the mules bring the miners' lift up and down, night and morning."

"I see. Thank you, Mr. Clegg. I'll be here tomorrow morning."

She walked staidly enough to the crest of the hill, but once over it she lifted her skirts a little and ran for a couple hundred feet. For the first time in six months, she felt almost light-hearted.

About a half-mile after she had turned onto the main road,

she climbed a low stone wall into a grassy field. Except for a small flock of grazing sheep a few hundred feet away, the field was empty. For a while she just sat there, enjoying the sunlight and the smell of long grass. Then, even though she knew from the sun's position that it was still short of noon, she ate her dinner of bread and cheese. After that she still sat there, dreaming of her and Jaimie's future. There was a village about two miles beyond the Fallon farm. Perhaps when she had saved enough, she could open some sort of shop there, with rooms above for herself and her little boy—

Finally she got to her feet, climbed over the wall, and walked on.

When she turned into the narrow road leading up to the Fallon house, she saw Flora coming toward her, wheeling the loaded handcart. They met in front of one of the pens. Still gripping the cart's handle, Flora stopped and said, "So they turned you away. What took you so long getting back here?"

"I wasn't turned away. I'm to be the new paymaster, starting tomorrow. Eight shillings a week."

Flora's jaw dropped slightly. Otherwise she was able to mask whatever chagrin she felt. After a long, silent moment she said, "You want to go on living here?"

Maryann already had decided that. Room and board in the village, if available at all, might be expensive. Besides, she did not want to break with Flora. The Fallons were the nearest thing she had to kinfolk. Furthermore, Flora was Jaimie's aunt, and co-inheritor of his grandmother's farm.

"Yes, if you'll let me."

"You'll have to pay for your keep. Two shillings a week. That's less than you'd pay anywhere else."

"All right. Two shillings."

9

In his office the next morning, the superintendent led her to a desk in one corner. "See that pile of letters? The fellow who had this job before wrote them. I sent some out, although maybe I shouldn't have, but these were too bad to even consider. See if you can rewrite them."

The letters were as bad as Clarence Clegg had said—misspelled, poorly punctuated, and sometimes illegible. Questioning Clegg on some point now and then, she worked several hours rewriting her predecessor's work. When she had finished about a dozen, he read them, approval showing on his face even though his only comment was that they would "do."

When the clock on the office wall pointed to noon, she heard the sound of a steam whistle. No one emerged from the mine's yawning mouth, though. Evidently the miners ate their dinners below.

She ate her bread and cheese and then went back to the

letters. When she had rewritten the last of them, Clegg handed her a sheet of paper. "Write a letter to the mine owners about this."

After frowning over the paper a few moments, she concluded that it was a list of matters to which Clegg wished to draw the mine owners' attention. "Water high in lower leg. tun." apparently meant that the deepest mine tunnels were partially flooded, or might become so. "Wind. cable worn" probably meant that the windlass cable should be renewed. She began to feel a certain sympathy for the previous paymaster-clerk. Surely part of the trouble was that Clegg himself didn't know how to present information in an orderly fashion.

Asking him a question now and then, she drew up the letter. This time he was less grudging in his praise.

In the late afternoon he showed her the list of miners' names posted beside the pay window, each followed by the amount of money due him for the week. A man's pay, he explained, depended upon the skill required for his particular job—men who set off dynamite blasts were among the highest paid—and the length of his time on the job. In a few cases deductions had been made for tardiness.

"Why are some of the miners paid only four shillings?"

"Oh, they're not miners. They draw the ore cars."

At seven o'clock the whistle again let out a long blast. Standing somewhat nervously at the pay window, she heard the creak of the windlass and saw the first two loads of men emerge from the lift. They moved toward the pay window. Aware of Clegg standing beside her and fearful of paying out the wrong amounts, she concentrated on the list posted beside the window and the coins in the till. Nevertheless, she was aware of the reaction in coal-blackened faces as she laid coins in calloused palms. Some looked astounded. Some, after thirteen hours below ground, apparently were too tired to feel anything but dull curiosity.

At last she murmured to Clegg, "None of the ore-car men have been paid."

"Oh, they come up last."

He looked at her, considering. All day he had felt a pull of attraction toward her. Oh, not that he intended to do anything about it. His wife, a woman of sharp tongue, would be difficult enough to live with after she heard the news. Besides, making an advance would almost surely lose him the best paymaster-clerk he had ever had.

Still, he could not resist the temptation to bring a blush to her cheek. Besides, she'd learn all about it sooner or later anyway.

He said, when she had paid the last of miners, "You see, the ones who draw the ore cars aren't men. They're girls."

"Girls!"

"Yes. The tunnels are small, just big enough for a miner to use his pickax lying on his back or side, or for a loaded ore car to get through. But whoever pulls the cars has to go on all fours and be pretty small. That's why they use girls instead of boys."

She asked, "How old are the girls?"

"Some about ten. Most of them twelve, fourteen, or a little older." He gave a sly smile. Eyes fastened on her face, he said, "It's hot down there. Besides, clothes might get caught under the wheels. So they work naked, except for a breechclout. There's a kind of harness that goes over their shoulders and back between their legs to fasten to the ore car."

He saw no blush. Instead, her face turned white.

He said uneasily, "They don't mind. After a while they get to be like animals."

The mine was disgorging them now, diminutive figures in dark dresses that reached to midcalf on some, to the ankles on others. So that was why they came up last. They had to cover their nakedness before appearing on the surface of the earth.

They were streaming toward her now. She saw that the tallest of these girls—no, not girls; children—would reach only to her shoulder, and she was not tall. As they held out their palms for the coins, she saw dull wonder in the exhausted faces streaked with coal dust.

The last girl, with coal-dusted yellow hair and eyes that looked startlingly blue in her dirty face, was less tall than some of the girls. Yet a certain weight of experience in the blue eyes made Maryann ask, "How old are you?"

"Eighteen, mum."

"How long have you been working here?"

"Since I was nine, mum."

Eighteen, and she was the size of a ten-year-old! Maryann had a vision of what she must have been like as an infant—a pretty creature with every promise of becoming a lovely young wife and mother. But who would want this wizened creature, dwarfed by half a lifetime of crawling almost naked through low tunnels, her thin shoulders dragging a load of coal?

For a few moments Maryann watched the girls moving away, some taking the path that crossed the crest, others taking the one that led past a long pile of tailings to the valley.

At last she turned to Clegg. "I won't be coming back tomorrow."

Struck speechless, he just looked at her.

"I can't stand the sight of those children." She had known that in many places children were employed in exhausting, dangerous jobs. In carpet factories, for instance, and textile mills. But never had she suspected that children were subjected to such degradation as this.

He had found his voice. "It's their parents that put them here! And damned glad they are of the extra shillings. What's it to do with you?"

It was simply that she could not sit here at a desk day after day, knowing that a few hundred feet below those dwarfed girls—

Far better to go on working at the pig farm.

"I'm sorry, Mr. Clegg, and I do thank you for the opportunity you gave me. But I can't stay. And so, if you will pay me for today—"

Loudly protesting, he gave her one shilling tuppence, and then followed her a little way along the ledge that led to the path over the hill. At last he stopped and shouted after her, "All right! But you'll be back! And maybe I'll hire you and maybe I won't."

Not turning, she walked up the slope.

10

She was feeding the pigs in a pen about a hundred yards from the house several mornings later when she heard the soft thud of hooves. She looked over her shoulder. Sir Rodney Athaire was riding toward her.

He stopped beside the pen. "Good morning, Mrs. Fallon."

So today she was not "lass."

She turned around. "Good morning, Sir Rodney."

Obviously he was trying not to look at her mud-splattered bare legs. "I hear you were paymaster up at the mine for a while a few days ago."

She said, astonished, "How is it you know that?"

"I stopped at an inn last night. Some men there were talking about it. They said it was learning about the ore-car girls that made you leave."

She nodded.

"Commendable, I'm sure. Shows a tender, womanly heart,

and all that." He paused. "I'd like to speak to your sister-in-law."

"I think you'll find her at the other side of the house, mixing feed."

He rode up the slope. When he returned, Maryann had just finished the feeding in another pan and, empty bucket in hand, was fastening the gate. Reining in beside her, Sir Rodney said, "As I think I told you, a lot of this land once belonged to an ancestor of mine. The other day in an old letter I ran across a reference to runic stones my ancestor found here. Do you know what runic stones are?"

"Stones with ancient writing carved on them?"

He nodded. "Usually in language of early Germanic origin. You seem quite knowledgeable, Mrs. Fallon."

She said, unsmiling, "Thank you." Somehow she was sure that runes were not the reason he had come here, or at least not the main reason.

"I've felt for some time that I owe you an apology for offering you a maid's position on my household staff."

Her voice was even. "No apology is necessary, Sir Rodney."

What a high-nosed bitch she was, this American woman, this woman who was too thin for his taste, and dark-haired rather than blond, and perhaps as much as ten years older than he liked them. The fifteen- and sixteen-year-olds seemed to believe him when, after a bout of amorous wrestling, he said, "You can go now. I find I'm not in the mood, after all." It was in the eyes of the older ones that he sometimes saw a flicker of amused contempt.

It must be that very high-nosed quality of hers that had kept her in his thoughts. What a pleasure it would be to bring her to unwilling submission, her clothing in disarray, her hair down her back.

He said, "But now that I know your true capabilities, I can offer you a position worthy of you. The men at the inn said that the mine superintendent, whatever his name is—"

"His name is Clarence Clegg."

"I heard them say that according to this Clegg, you had the makings of a first-rate clerk. Now as it happens, my wife has been complaining that she needs a secretary. For once, I agree with her. My steward—or rather, assistant steward—has repeatedly urged her to keep some sort of record of her expenditures, but it does no good. She says she has no head for figures. Also, she finds it burdensome to keep up with the social correspondence commensurate with her position, although I have observed that many ladies of my acquaintance are enthusiastic letter writers."

His wife's two enthusiasms, he reflected, were spending money on clothes and jewels and spending time with Jonathan Burke. He'd long since stopped minding Jonathan. But he did mind the money she spent.

"Your salary would be thirty pounds a year, plus, of course, your keep."

Thirty pounds! More than she would make if she had remained in Clegg's employ—much, much more if you figured in her board and room. And she would be living in that beautiful house. She pictured it as she had seen it from the jolting cart, spilling lamplight from tall windows onto a misty lake.

"Consider it for a day or two," he said. "Next Wednesday, say, I will send a messenger for your answer."

"I'm quite sure my answer will be yes."

"Splendid! Of course," he added, in a casual tone, "you will be expected to be affable to other members of the family."

She knew exactly what he meant. "I always try to be affable," she said. Her eyes added coldly, But affability is all you will get from me.

His smile seemed to say, Would you care to wager that? Aloud he said, "Good day, Mrs. Fallon. I shall send that messenger."

Heart beating fast, she pushed the cart up the slope. Flora still stood beside the buckets, stirring their contents with the long paddle. She said, "Offered you a place again, didn't he?"

Flora was smiling. After a moment Maryann realized it was not a sardonic smile. Instead, Flora was manifesting more warmth—or at least trying to—than Maryann had observed in her until now.

"Yes, a splendid place, secretary to her ladyship. Thirty pounds a year."

"No!" Then, urgently: "Take it, Maryann. You'll never get another chance like that. I'll miss your help, but I can get along without you. Just think! Secretary to her ladyship. Why, you'll be more like a member of the family than a servant."

Maryann understood then. Money had changed hands. Just how much, she wondered, had Sir Rodney paid Flora to urge his case? It must have taken more than a pound or two to make Flora feel compensated for the loss of her sister-in-law's labor.

For a moment she had a sense of foreboding, as if she

were about to step into a world more complicated and more dangerous than any she had ever known. But why should she feel that? Flora had said that all Sir Rodney was capable of was "a slap and a tickle." Surely a woman in her twenties could ward off an aging, impotent fumbler.

And yet there was this strange uneasiness. . . .

She shoved it aside. Windmere meant cleanliness instead of noxious mud, a soft bed instead of a cornhusk mattress. And best of all, money. Money to build a future for Jaimie, that child who was doubly precious because he was all of Donald that was left upon this earth.

"I've already decided to accept Sir Rodney's offer," Maryann said.

11

Tom Lothar, the Athaire coachman, was in a quandary. When he had been given orders early that morning to fetch "a young woman" from the Fallon farm, he had pictured one of Sir Rodney's usual poppets—blond, bouncy, and giggly. In fact, he had planned to boost the girl up onto the box beside him and keep her there until they were within a mile or so of Windmere.

But when he reached the Fallon place—phew, what a smell!—and saw the young woman awaiting him in front of the house, his plans changed. Who was she, this woman in her cloak and bonnet of severe black? Surely not one of Sir Rodney's choices as a plaything.

He got down from the high seat. "I'm Lothar, ma'am, Sir Rodney's coachman."

"I'm Mrs. Fallon."

He helped her into the coach and placed her portmanteau beside her feet. When the coach turned and started down the slope, Maryann looked back. Donald's mother was waving forlornly from her window. Although Flora had taken her sister-in-law's departure cheerfully enough—so cheerfully that Maryann had raised her estimate of how much Sir Rodney had paid her—Mrs. Fallon had been devastated. "It's no place for you," she wept. "They say strange things go on at Windmere."

"What things?"

"Sir Rodney—bothers servant girls."

"From what I have heard," Maryann said dryly, "bothering servant girls is not such strange behavior for a man in his position. Besides, I can watch out for myself."

"But folks say there are other queer things going on!"

"What things?"

"Oh," she said, "just things." Then she burst out, "You'll never come back! I'll never get to see my grandson!"

So that was her greatest fear. "But you will! You'll see him even sooner this way. I'm going to make an excellent salary, Mother Fallon. And I'm going to save every bit of it that I can."

Now, early in the afternoon, the coach moved down the sloping road toward the tall house beside the lake.

Lothar frowned. Which entrance? When he set out on his journey that morning, he of course had intended to leave his passenger at the servants' entrance. Perhaps he still should. After all, Mr. Cramer, who had passed Sir Rodney's orders on to him, had said "young woman," not "young lady." And yet the woman inside the coach looked every inch a lady—widowed, American, and poor, to judge by the quality of her attire, but a lady.

Perhaps, unlikely as that seemed, Mr. Cramer had misunderstood his instructions from Sir Rodney. Anyway, he would leave her at the front entrance.

As he pulled up at the foot of the semicircular steps of gray stone, no footman emerged to hurry down to the carriage. That was an ominous sign that no guest had been expected. Nevertheless, the coachman got down and opened the door for her. He set her portmanteau beside her on the lowest step, gave her a hurried salute, climbed onto the box, and drove around the corner of the house toward the stables.

When she was halfway up the steps, the door did open and a man in a bottle-green coat and brown riding breeches and boots came out. At the sight of her he stopped short. He said, sounding puzzled and surprised, "Good afternoon."

"Good afternoon." Then, since an explanation seemed to be necessary: "I'm Mrs. Fallon, Maryann Fallon. I've been engaged as Lady Athaire's secretary."

Martin Cramer felt astounded. Sir Rodney's taste had undergone a radical change. Not that this girl wasn't attractive. She was, very much so. That lustrous dark hair showing from under her bonnet. The big brown eyes under well-defined brows. The full mouth that looked all the more voluptuous because of the thinness of her high-cheekboned face.

But she looked like no one who would interest Sir Rodney. Yet here she was, not only decidedly unplump and unblond, but a widow—or at least she had gotten herself up to pass for one. As unlikely a candidate as she seemed for Sir Rodney's hole-in-the-corner games, that must be why she was there. Sir Rodney was the one who had sent for her, not his wife.

He said, "How do you do, Mrs. Fallon? I'm Martin Cramer, the assistant steward here at Windmere." His tone was polite, but she could see the contempt in his eyes, gray eyes set in a bony, rather sardonic face. She looked back at him coldly. "How do you do?"

"Let me carry this for you."

He picked up the portmanteau and climbed beside her up the steps. She noticed that he limped slightly.

Now the double doors, made of etched glass and set behind iron grilles, opened again. A tall young footman bowed to them. In his knee breeches and white wig, he looked as if he had stepped out of an eighteenth-century painting. As she stepped over the threshold, Maryann had an impression of a spacious hall, floored in black and white marble, with a staircase sweeping upward. No paintings hung on the paneled walls. Instead, statues of youth and maidens in classical Greek attire stood in niches. Through an open doorway she could see what was apparently the salon, a vast room filled with crystal chandeliers, thick carpets, and French furniture, most of it upholstered in yellow satin.

Martin said, "This is Mrs. Fallon, Patrick, who is to be secretary to her ladyship."

Again Patrick bowed.

"Show her into the library, Patrick, and then go tell her ladyship that Mrs. Fallon has arrived." Again he looked at Maryann with those gray, sardonic eyes. She wondered how old he was. Thirty-three? A little older?

"Good day, Mrs. Fallon." Again aware of that half-veiled contempt in his manner, she lifted her chin and said, "Good day, Mr. Cramer."

He turned and went out the front door.

Maryann followed the footman across the hall to a set of massively carved double doors. He opened one of the doors, bowed her inside, closed the door behind her. She took a few steps over the carpet, then stood motionless.

Her heart, too, seemed to stand still in her breast.

Donald.

Donald was standing across the room. His back was turned to her as he looked out a window framed with dark red velvet draperies, but he was Donald. There was no mistaking the shape of that beloved head with its cap of yellow hair, the set of those broad shoulders in a gray broadcloth coat.

Her heart, no longer still, pounded with hysterical joy.

So it had all been a long, terrible dream. His death in the icy road. Her long, lonely voyage, the weeks on the Fallon farm.

All a dream. None of it could have happened because her husband was *alive*.

He turned. He *was* Donald. The sea-blue eyes. The handsome face with its straight, rather blunt nose, its well-cut mouth with the full lower lip, the square chin.

Smiling, he moved toward her. He said, "And who are *you*?"

He was very close to her now, almost looming over her. A terrible anguish, followed by a nameless fear, seemed to twist everything inside her.

Because he was not her husband. He looked almost exactly like him, even sounded a little like him, but he was not Donald.

Instead, he was something evil.

She could see the evil peering out at her from the bright blue eyes, the wide smile.

The room seemed to swim around her.

72

12

"I say! You're not going to faint, are you? You had best sit down."

His hand fastened around her arm and led her to a straight chair against the wall. She sat. That instinctive fear was gone now. All she felt was pain. It was like a second bereavement, in some ways even more anguished than the first.

"You look as if you need a brandy."

He crossed the room, tall and perfectly groomed in his fine broadcloth coat and trousers—garments surely more expensive than any Donald had ever worn in his whole life—and knelt on one knee before a rosewood liquor cabinet. Vaguely she was aware of thick brown carpeting, a gleaming refectory table, bookshelves rising almost to the high ceiling. He came back with a brandy glass containing amber liquid. "Drink this."

The brandy stung her throat, burned in her stomach.

But it stopped that feeling that she might pitch forward to the floor. And perhaps it brought her to her senses, at least enough that she realized that this man was younger by several years than Donald had been. There were no fine lines at the corners of his eyes, no crease in the broad forehead. He was perfection, like a Michelangelo statue of the young David.

He took the empty glass, set it on the refectory table, and came back to stand before her. "Are you Lady Athaire's secretary, the one Sir Rodney hired?"

She nodded. "I'm Mrs. Fallon," she managed to say. "Maryann Fallon."

What, he wondered, had possessed the old boy? She was not at all like the buxom young trollops he usually chose for his impotent fumblings. Could it be that she really was good at correspondence and keeping accounts? He hoped so. Elaine was always trying to get him to figure out how much of her dress allowance was left, and just how she should answer the Princess Brunelli's letter, and so on.

He said, "My name is Jonathan Burke. I am Sir Rodney's steward."

His steward, the manager of the Athaire estate. It was returning now, that indefinable sense of Jonathan Burke's essential evil. Maryann wondered that any landholder would trust this man to run his affairs.

"Feeling better? You have some color in your face now." She was damned lovely, in spite of that hideous black clothing.

"Yes, I'm much better."

"Very well. I will tell Lady Athaire that you are here, and then take you to her."

He left the room.

She looked down at her clasped hands. Who was he? Until she realized that he was several years younger than Donald had been, she had thought he might be her husband's twin. Certainly they must be kinsmen. True, there was an old saying that everyone, somewhere on earth, had a "double," someone entirely unrelated to him by blood. But it was absurd to surmise that she would find such a double of Donald's living in this splendid house only a few miles from the farm where her husband had been born.

And so what was the relationship of this evilly beautiful man to her lost beloved?

She was looking vaguely at a portrait above the marble fireplace of a beplumed Cavalier—the first baronet, perhaps?—when Jonathan Burke came back into the room. "Lady Athaire will see you now, Mrs. Fallon."

She accompanied him out into the hall and up sweeping, marble-balustraded stairs. The air was faintly fragrant with the mingled scent of fresh flowers, beeswax furniture polish, and the wax tapers that must have burned in the wall sconces the night before. At the landing he led her down a narrower hall, knocked briefly on a door, then opened it and stepped back for her to pass in front of him into a sitting room. Rose-filled crystal vases stood on small tables beside a love seat and an easy chair. On the wall hung a large, silver-framed mounting of iridescent blue butterflies.

Jonathan Burke had moved ahead of her to stand sideways in an inner doorway. "Lady Athaire, Mrs. Fallon is here."

Maryann stepped past him into a room that was sheer luxury. A painted ceiling where winged cupids sported among clouds drifting across a blue sky. A huge four-poster bed with green satin hangings. A flowered rug that sank underfoot. More roses. And butterflies everywhere. Embroidered ones on the bed hangings and on sofa cushions adorning Louis Quinze chairs. Once-living ones—blue, green, orange, multicolored—preserved in small glass-covered frames on the littered dressing table and on various small stands around the room.

A woman Maryann knew must be Lady Athaire lay on a chaise longue covered with green-and-silver-striped satin. Her eyes were green and slightly tilted. Her hair was red, caught at the nape of the neck and spilling in ringlets over her shoulders. Her yellow satin gown was cut so low over her swelling breasts that Maryann was reminded of reproductions she had seen of paintings by Lely of Charles II's mistresses. She looked quite beautiful and not more than forty-two or -three. Maryann was to learn later that she was at least a decade older. Perhaps it was creams and lotions, as well as recourse to dyes and rouge pots, that accounted for her youthful appearance.

Stretched out across the foot of the chaise was a silver Persian cat, its plumy tail waving, its eyes regarding Maryann with indifference.

Lady Athaire said, waving a white, rather plump hand toward a small armchair, "How do you do, Mrs. Fallon? Sit there, please," Then: "That will be all for now, Mr. Burke." She usually called him that when others were near.

When they were alone, she smiled and said, "So you are the young woman Sir Rodney selected to keep my accounts. Tell me, did you actually serve a day as paymaster at a mine?"

"Yes, Lady Athaire."

"My husband told me that that was how he had heard of you, but I thought that perhaps that was just one of his jokes. Well," she went on, "I'm sure that keeping track of my little expenditures will be much easier than being pay-master at a mine."

She had a vague hope that this quiet-looking but appar-ently very clever Mrs. Fallon would think of a few more ways of concealing her purchases from her husband—or rather, from that awful Martin Cramer. *He* was the one who had insisted that there be a record of her expenditures. Often she imagined herself saying to him, "I shall insist that my husband dismiss you."

But that speech would have to remain a fantasy. If it were not for Cramer, Jonathan would have to be—or at least *try* to be—the estate's steward in fact as well as title. For her that would mean far fewer hours spent playing cards with Jonathan and riding to their trysting place, an old, long-unused hunting lodge deep in the woods. Instead, Jonathan would have to try to concern himself with rents and taxes and repairs and sheep and cattle. (The cattle breeding, she vaguely remembered hearing, was Martin Cramer's idea. He was trying to develop a new breed or something like that.)

She said, "Did Sir Rodney tell you you would also be expected to handle my correspondence?"

"Yes, Lady Athaire."

"I find writing letters such a bore!"

The truth was that she found writing letters—or trying to—both onerous and humiliating.

She had been born Elaine Blodgett, above a dyer's shop

77

in London, two months after her parents, both eighteen, had married at the registry office.

If Elaine's father had been a rash young man in some ways, he had been in others both hardworking and inventive. Fourteen hours a day he had labored among the dye vats in the shop, which belonged to his father. After supper he would return to the shop and experiment with various combinations of chemicals.

Less than a year after his father's death, he had concocted a dye that was both colorfast and cheaper to make than anything on the market. He took it to a friend of his father's, an ex-dyer who had prospered enough to set up his own dye-manufacturing company.

It was Blodgett's good fortune that his father's old friend was an honest man. The manufacturer could have offered a hundred pounds for the formula, and the young man would have accepted gladly. Instead, the older man helped Blodgett take out a patent.

Within a year, the Blodgetts were on their way to being rich. Within ten years, advertisements for Blodgett's Dyes ornamented London's horse-drawn omnibuses and appeared in periodicals throughout the British Isles and in Europe.

Elaine was eight when the money began to flood in. Her parents knew that it was too late for them, even though they were still only twenty-six. No matter what sort of London mansion they bought or how richly they dressed, their origins would show in their speech and manner. But their beautiful red-haired daughter could be made into a fine lady.

They hired the impoverished widow of a high Anglican

clergyman to drill and drill the little girl until she stopped dropping her aitches. They hired a dancing master and a piano teacher. They managed to get her into a fairly good boarding school and then, after a year, into a better one. Finally, by making a large contribution of its building restoration fund, they were able to enroll her in Medford Academy in Kent, one of the best finishing schools near London.

But although she had learned how to speak and walk and sit, how to use a fish knife and maneuver a fan, she had never learned how to express herself on paper or even how to achieve a graceful handwriting—and this at a time when most upper-class women, including the Queen, spent a lot of time diary-keeping and letter-writing.

When Rodney Athaire first saw her at a country house party, he neither knew nor cared if she could write a line. He was thirty then, and she a few months short of eighteen.

If the third baronet had been alive, he doubtless would have interfered. But he had been dead two years. And so Sir Rodney, as the fourth baronet, went to Blodgett and asked if he might sue for his daughter's hand.

The Blodgetts were delighted. Elaine did not like Sir Rodney very much—already he tended toward plumpness and baldness—but she loved the sound of *Lady Athaire*.

Both Sir Rodney and his wife now felt that their union had turned out fairly well. True, their first child, a girl, had not arrived until the sixth year of their marriage, and she had not lived past infancy. They had remained childless for several years, but finally, when she was thirty-eight, Elaine had produced the son and heir.

After the birth Sir Rodney seemed to lose interest in

visiting Lady Athaire's bed. Elaine did not mind, nor was she surprised when she heard that her husband was pursuing servant girls, although she did feel vaguely sorry for one of them, an upstairs maid named Milly who, big with child, had to be sent home to her textile-worker parents. After a while she learned that Windmere housemaids no longer needed to fear Milly's fate. Sir Rodney still pursued female servants, but when he caught them, all that ensued was a little amorous tussling.

Lady Athaire learned this in the usual roundabout fashion. Maids at Windmere, meeting on their days off with servants from other establishments, talked about Sir Rodney. Finally a lady's maid told her mistress, who told other women of her circle. Eventually one of them told Elaine.

She had received the news with little interest. She really didn't care what her husband did or didn't do, as long as he did not interfere with her and Jonathan.

Maryann said, "Yes, Sir Rodney explained that there would be letters to write."

"And you settled upon your salary."

"We did."

"Then I suppose that's really all—oh! I haven't introduced you to Pompom, have I?" With one yellow-slippered foot she stroked the side of the silver Persian. "He's naughty, Pompom is. He gets away and runs to those dreadful old tomcats in the stables and comes back with his beautiful fur all torn and awful-looking."

The Persian had narrowed his eyes and flattened his ears, as if he disliked being stroked with a slipper, disliked his silly name, and intended to seek the companionship of the stable toms at the first opportunity.

"I'll have Mrs. Burnbeck show you to your quarters."

She reached for the bellrope hanging on the wall. "Mrs. Burnbeck is the housekeeper."

"Please, Lady Athaire. Just a moment." Then as the woman, looking startled, took her hand away from the bellrope: "Could you tell me who Jonathan Burke is?"

"Why, didn't he tell you? He's my husband's steward."

"Yes, he told me that. But where does he come from?"

Lady Athaire's green eyes narrowed slightly. Perhaps she did not want this young woman's services. The presumption of her, asking where Jonathan came from!

Had this American woman been smitten with him at first sight? Lady Athaire could well understand that.

But surely Jonathan would not reciprocate. Oh, the American was somewhat nice-looking in a mousy, underfed way. But that was not what Jonathan wanted. He had told Elaine often enough what he wanted in a woman, had always wanted: Green eyes. Red hair. A tiny waist emphasizing the swell of breasts and hips.

She said coldly, "His people were quite humble. Green-grocers, in a town called Marly-on-Willowbrook."

"I've never heard of it."

"Of course you haven't. It's a small place about ten miles from York on the railroad line. As for Jonathan, a kind benefactor sent him to Winchester and then on to Oxford. Awhile after that he came to us. Why do you ask?"

"He is almost a double of someone."

"A double? Of someone you know?"

Maryann almost said, "My late husband." But she checked herself. Better not to be too confiding until she knew more about the people here, more about this place, which was proving to be, in her mother-in-law's word, "strange."

But she was going to stay here. Donald had been related

to this Jonathan Burke. He had to be. Which meant that he was related to Jaimie. For the sake of her and Donald's son, she had to learn the truth.

"Someone I knew in America," she said. "He looked so much like Mr. Burke that I thought they might be related."

"Related? To an American?" She laughed. "I scarcely think so."

Again she started to reach for the bellrope, then hesitated. "Oh, there is one thing more. It's rather awkward."

"Oh?"

"It's about the meals. Mr. Burke and Mr. Cramer dine with Sir Rodney and me. And of course there is the servants' hall—"

She broke off, looking confused. Maryann thought, with something like pity, Why, she isn't well-bred at all, in spite of her money and her title. She is awkward and untactful.

Maryann said aloud, "Is it that you feel it would not be proper for me to dine either place, either with you and Sir Rodney or with the servants?"

Lady Athaire looked relieved. "Yes. You see, I never had a personal secretary before."

"Why shouldn't I take my meals in my own room?"

"Of course!" Elaine Athaire cried. "I've assigned you a sitting room as well as a bedroom. You should be very comfortable. I'll call Mrs. Burnbeck now." She pulled the bellrope.

13

The sitting room and bedroom were small and shabby, the rugs threadbare in spots, the green muslin draperies skimpy, the white paint on the iron bedstead cracked and chipped. The plain white pitcher and basin on the corner washstand also bore hairline cracks. But Maryann did not mind, any more than she minded the extra flight of steps or the fact that she had been assigned to what was obviously the servants' floor. All this space to herself, after that tiny, low-ceilinged room at the Fallon farm. And these two windows in the bedroom, a corner room, with the red-gold sunset light flooding in.

She cried, "Oh, how nice everything is!"

Mrs. Burnback gave an almost audible sniff. She was a large woman with prominent brown eyes. "When I came here three years ago, they wanted me to take these rooms, but I said I preferred to be at the front of the house. I told them I was used to nicer furnishings, too."

Although she had never even been inside the doors of a multiservanted household, with all its jostling for status among the staff members, Maryann could tell that Mrs. Burnbeck was a little worried. Would this American feel that she outranked a housekeeper, who had the entire household staff at her command?

Maryann said with a placating smile, "I'm sure yours are much nicer, but these will do very well for me."

Mrs. Burnbeck looked at Maryann's portmanteau. Plainly, someone had brought it up from the entrance hall and placed it beside the old oak armoire in this room. "I suppose your trunk will arrive later."

Maryann felt embarrassed warmth in her cheeks. "I'm afraid that is all the baggage I have."

She knew that her extremely limited wardrobe, which had been adequate for the farm, wouldn't do for even an upper servant in this house. Well, she was handy with a needle. Most of her salary would go to the Yerxas to pay for Jaimie's keep and for his eventual voyage to join her. But she would also spend a few shillings for dress material.

Mrs. Burnback said, "Your dinner will be served at seven-thirty. Your breakfast will be brought at seven. I don't know about your luncheon. Perhaps you may serve yourself from the dining-room buffet. I'll ask Lady Athaire. Oh! And your tea. It will be served up here at five."

After a pause she added, "There is a WC down the hall."

She walked out of the bedroom into the sitting room. The hall door closed behind her.

By the time Maryann had hung her meager wardrobe in the old armoire and tidied her hair and washed her face, the sun had set and the long twilight had begun. From the western window of her bedroom she could see down into a formal garden. Its gravel path was bordered by bushes laden with roses ranging in color from deep red to pure white. At various points, shining glass balls atop marble pedestals gave back a miniaturized version of the roses. The main path ran from the house to a white pavilion set against a boxwood hedge.

She moved to the south window. From there, beyond the hedge that enclosed the garden area, she could see low brick buildings that evidently housed the stables. Two young boys, each with a bucket beside him, were currying what appeared to be the matched pair of dappled grays that had brought her from the Fallon farm.

Again she went to the west window and looked down at those riotously blooming roses. Then she went into the sitting room and looked at the clock on the mantelpiece, a china clock supported by cupids, one of which had lost half a wing. Almost seven-thirty. Nevertheless, she could not resist the thought of a quick trip through that beautiful garden.

Front or back stairs? Front, she decided, even though the back stairs were closer. Mrs. Burnbeck had brought her up the front stairs, although whether she had acted out of deference to her own position rather than that of Lady Athaire's secretary, Maryann had no idea.

She descended through the silent house. She saw no one until she reached the ground floor, where the same tall young footman who had admitted her to the house was lighting the tapers in their wall sconces. He said, "Good evening, ma'am."

"Good evening. Is the entrance to the garden this way?"

"Yes, just keep going, ma'am."

She moved through the flickering light of scented tapers, mirrored by the polished, paneled walls, to the double doors at the hall's end. A brass doorknob turned under her hand, and she stepped out onto a flagstoned terrace set with white wicker chairs and small matching tables.

The gravel crunched under her feet. She drew in deep breaths of the cooling, rose-scented air. In one of the mirror-balls she saw her own distorted reflection, a tiny figure in somber black amid the riotously colored roses.

The octagonal pavilion had an umbrella roof of some sort of green-painted metal, supported by white wooden uprights. Except for a waist-high enclosure, also white, of elaborately carved wood, the eight-sided structure was open to the weather.

She climbed three low steps and sat down on the bench that ran around the building's interior. She realized that if not for Jonathan Burke, she might, at least for a few minutes, have felt almost content sitting here in the summer day's afterglow. But there *was* Jonathan Burke, that man who was almost a mirror-image of Donald Fallon and yet, she was somehow sure, lacked all the qualities that had made her love Donald—kindness, courage, and a good humor that had been proof against nearly all of life's everyday vexations.

A movement to her left, glimpsed from the corner of her eye. Quite suddenly, someone was standing there, someone who must have crouched behind the waist-high enclosure and then gotten to his feet. Already feeling a sick dread, she turned her head.

He was small, almost a dwarf, with a large head covered

86

with woolly black hair. A hideous head, gray eyes bulging, nose short with huge nostrils, almost like a pig's snout, the grin wide and toothless, the chin ornamented with a wart.

She sat paralyzed, speechless. Then she saw him move, saw that he was coming around to the pavilion's entrance. Paralysis left her. She rose, bolted for the narrow exit.

On the second step her skirts tripped her. She pitched forward onto the graveled path.

For a moment she lay with the breath knocked out of her. Then she raised her head, placed her palms on the gravel to lift herself—

His grotesque head rising above a ragged dark cloak, he stood two or three feet away on the path, looking down at her.

She managed to scream then, but it was the kind of scream one gives in a nightmare, the throat so thick with terror that the sound is strangled, not nearly loud enough for anyone inside the house to hear.

But someone outside the house had heard. He came through the low gate in the hedge that separated the rose garden from the stable area. Almost running, he came down a side path, turned onto the main one.

The dwarf was aware of the newcomer now. He turned, tried to dodge away through the rose bushes. Martin Cramer's grasp fastened onto the collar of the cloak. "Luddy, you blasted she-devil!"

She-devil? A mask, then? Even as the thought was crossing Maryann's mind, Martin ripped off the mask, dropped it onto the gravel. Then he reached down and helped Maryann to her feet.

He still held the cloaked figure by the collar. She *was* a

woman, Maryann saw now, a thin little woman about five feet tall. Her hair, which looked as if it had never known a comb or brush, was grayish brown. In contrast to that hideous mask, her real face looked almost appealing, like that of a wizened child. A sheepish grin added to the child-like quality. Impossible to tell her age. She might have been anywhere from forty to sixty.

Still holding her, Martin kicked at the mask with a booted toe. "When did you get that, Luddy? The fun fair last May?"

The gray-brown head ducked an assent.

"Pick it up."

He released her. The cloaked figure stooped.

"Now tear it up."

Woe washed over the wizened face.

"I mean it, Luddy."

The mask must have been made of papier-mâché except for the woollike black hair, because the woman's grubby fingers seemed to have no trouble ripping it apart.

"No! Don't leave all that litter on the path. Take it with you!"

Luddy gathered up the pieces and stored them in some recess beneath the ragged cloak.

Martin's voice was stern. "You don't want to go back to the madhouse, do you?"

Terror crossed her face. "Oh, no, sir. Oh, no!"

"Then behave yourself. Stop playing tricks. You might have caused Mrs. Fallon to hurt herself." He looked at Maryann. "Are you hurt?"

"No." Her palms stung because she had used her hands to break her fall onto the gravel. Otherwise, she seemed to be all right.

He returned his attention to Luddy. "Now go. Use the back gate in the hedge. And don't come back. Stay away from here, if you know what's good for you."

The small figure scurried around the pavilion. Maryann heard a gate creak open, then close with a click.

Reaction had set in. Maryann began to tremble all over. Martin said, taking her arm, "I'll help you into the house." Then he paused, frowning down at her. "You're white as a sheet. You'd better sit down for a moment."

They sat on the bench in the pavilion. She asked, "Who is Luddy?"

"Nobody knows, really. She tells all sorts of conflicting stories about herself, the most likely one being that she ran away from a family of tinkers camped near Lancashire and gradually made her way to this area. She thinks she was about twelve when she ran away."

"Has she really been in a madhouse?"

"For a short time. Some kindly souls who were tired of seeing her around demanded that she be sent to the asylum near York. When the asylum became overcrowded, the doctors there let Luddy go. She isn't really dangerous, you know. Just a nuisance. She'll even work for a few days now and then, picking apples or carding wool. The rest of the time she begs. Probably steals a little, too."

"How old is she?"

"Who knows? Some people say she's been around here for thirty years or more and that she was grown—at least physically—when she first appeared."

"There was a man like that back in my Connecticut village. People tolerated him, even though he was a problem sometimes."

"Connecticut. That's on the eastern coast of America, isn't it?"

She nodded.

"Tell me, have you ever been to the American West? Texas, say?"

"No. Until I came to England, I had never traveled more than twenty miles from where I was born."

He sounded disappointed. "I see."

For a moment there was silence. Again he wondered how it was that Sir Rodney, with his tastes, had brought this young woman here. Perhaps—

He said, "How is it that you were chosen to do secretarial work for Lady Athaire?"

She explained about her day at the mine. "Sir Rodney heard about it at some inn, and so he came to my sister-in-law's house—my mother-in-law's, actually—and asked if I would like to keep Lady Athaire's accounts and handle her correspondence."

So perhaps it *was* just because of her ability that she had been hired. Martin felt relief so sharp that it surprised him.

"You and Sir Rodney had not met before that?"

"Yes. He came to the Fallon farm several weeks ago. He said that his family used to own that land before some ancestor sold it."

So he had seen her before he took the notion of hiring her. "That first time he came to the Fallon farm. Did he offer you employment then?"

Sensing the reason for the question, she looked at him coldly. She wanted to tell him that that was scarcely any concern of his. But after all, he could find out the truth one way or the other.

"Yes. He offered me a position as parlormaid, with a chance of becoming Lady Athaire's personal maid later on. I declined it."

He gave a slight, cynical smile. So she had waited until Sir Rodney had raised his offering price, and then accepted. One thing was clear. She was clever at more than just clerical work.

She asked evenly, "May I ask how it is that you attained your position?"

"As assistant to Jonathan Burke? I was his tutor for a year at Oxford."

"A tutor! You were a schoolmaster?"

"In a way. Before that I was a soldier, and before that an Oxford undergraduate. How are you feeling now?"

"Very well, thank you. Quite able to go to my room."

He stood up. "Splendid. Then I'll escort you into the house."

14

Maryann's supper was waiting for her in her sitting room. The tray sat on an old drop-leaf table in the glow of the gas jet just inside her door. Beneath the dented cover of a silver dish she found sliced lamb, whipped potatoes, and green peas, all quite good even though only lukewarm. In a little crock there was a sweet, some kind of bread pudding. She did not like it much but, not wanting to risk an offense to the cook, managed to eat it all.

Should she venture down to the belowstairs regions and leave her tray in the kitchen? Instinct told her that would be the wrong thing to do. She set the tray and its empty dishes on the hall floor outside her door. Then she went to the window and looked down through the gathering dusk at the pavilion.

She thought of Martin Cramer. He was not what you would call a charming man, but from the first she had felt a certain respect for him. It was plain, she thought wryly, that the respect was not returned. In his eyes, she was little more than another of Sir Rodney's strumpets. Well, perhaps in time Martin Cramer would realize that he was wrong about that. Anyway, did it matter much? What did matter was this opportunity to make and save money far more rapidly than she had expected to.

Even so, her thoughts returned to Martin Cramer. What had caused his limp? And why did he ask that question about Texas?

In the big dining room on the ground floor, gas jets flared on the paneled walls between full-length portraits of women in farthingales, men in doublet and hose, and velvet-clad young boys who managed to look haughty despite their childishly round faces framed in long ringlets. But in the crystal chandelier above the long oval table scented tapers burned, just as they had a hundred and fifty years ago when the first baron had built this house.

Sir Rodney sat at the head of the table. His face was flushed from the sherry that had accompanied the soup. A freckle-faced young footman who stood behind his chair had replenished his glass twice. By the time the dinner progressed to dessert and its accompanying port wine, he would have become a little incoherent. And soon after his wife had left him and Burke and Cramer to their brandy, he would be unsteady enough to need the footman to help him rise from his chair.

Lady Athaire sat at the other end of the table, clad in silk of her favorite color, yellow. Ornamenting her elaborately dressed red hair was Sir Rodney's first anniversary gift to her, a butterfly made of small diamonds and rubies and emeralds.

Jonathan Burke, seated at Elaine's right halfway along

the table, thought that after dinner, when he joined her in her sitting room, he would suggest a game of bezique. He needed money to make up for losses he had suffered three days earlier, when he played baccarat at his club in London. A few hours from now, he could be sure, Elaine would open the little safe behind the Greuze portrait in her sitting room and, with a pretty pout, lay four or five pounds on his outstretched palm.

Not that he always won. He let her win often enough to keep the words *card cheat* from crossing her mind.

But what about this Mrs. Fallon whom Sir Rodney had hired? Would *she* wonder why Lady Athaire lost so much of her allowance to her husband's steward?

Well, he thought with an inward smile, there were ways of handling the American widow. (The word *handling* brought such a graphic and amusing scene to his mind that he almost smiled openly.) He would have to be careful, because Elaine, lazily indifferent in most matters, could turn into a jealous wildcat where he was concerned. But he would manage somehow. Soon this Mrs. Fallon would not care what he did, as long as she could remain near him.

Martin Cramer, seated on her ladyship's left, was listening to her account of something she had read in *Whispers*, a new and more scurrilous rival of the London *Tatler*. It seemed that one of the Queen's maids-in-waiting, while on a trip to Italy, had tried to elope with an actor, a member of a company that played in Roman streets for coin-tossing spectators. Her parents had discovered—and scotched—her plans at the last moment.

Martin smiled. "From what I hear of the court's dullness these days, it is a wonder more of those young ladies don't elope."

He was listening with only part of his mind. That was a trick he had mastered since coming to Windmere. He could listen to Lady Athaire's chatter, and Jonathan Burke's quips, and Sir Rodney's occasional remarks, increasingly incoherent as the meal progressed. He could even contribute to the conversation. And all without interrupting his unvoiced thoughts.

Right now he too—somewhat to his annoyance—was thinking of Maryann Fallon. She was really worse than any of the trollops Sir Rodney had brought here. She was obviously a young woman of intelligence and some education. Surely she could get by without catering to the fumbling lusts of an aging sot.

Well, it was none of his business, Martin told himself. His business was to run this estate and, in return, receive a good part of the steward's salary paid to Jonathan. (Sometimes Martin wondered if Sir Rodney knew that his steward's supposed assistant did ninety percent of the work. Perhaps. Perhaps it didn't matter to him as long as the tenant farms paid their rent and Windmere didn't fall down around his ears and his wife's expenditures did not become so extreme that he had to curtail his own extravagances.)

Anyway, Martin reminded himself, it was foolish to worry about the actions or motives of anyone else beneath this roof. He intended to forge on toward his own goals.

Most of his life, it seemed to him, he had let others set his goals. Born to a fairly prosperous sheep farmer, he had spent a happy childhood in the Yorkshire dales. If he had followed his own inclinations, he would have stayed on the farm, working beside his father until the elder Cramer's death. But Martin's mother had had other plans. She was of higher social status than her husband—her mother had been related to minor gentry—and although she loved her sheep-farmer spouse, she had other ambitions for her son. She wanted him to follow the law. Consequently, he did not attend the village school. Instead, his parents managed to send him to a public school fifty miles away. Spurred on by his mother, he did so well in his classes that he won a scholarship to Oxford.

During his first long vacation from Oxford, he worked with his father's sheep. In his spare time, he rode horseback through the dales. One morning he rode past land that, he knew, had recently been bought by a rich London trades-man.

In one of the fields, amid the placidly grazing sheep, stood a creature of a sort Martin had never seen until now. It was a bull, long and lean, with a horn-spread about twice as wide as that of other cattle. A stout rope and an iron stake kept the animal tethered.

Martin stopped and talked to the sheepherder. The bull was a "longhorn," he said, and the Londoner had imported it as a novelty from Texas.

Martin knew where Texas was. Once part of Mexico, it had been annexed by the United States after the recent Mexican War. These cattle, the Londoner had told his herdsman, were remarkable for more than their appear-ance. They could live off almost any sort of vegetation. They had the stamina to endure thousand-mile treks without too much weight loss. The trouble was that their meat was tough, and the cows weren't good milkers.

Martin's voice was tense, "Has anyone in America tried to crossbreed them?"

The herdsman shrugged. How could he know what went

on in America, a land so distant that he wasn't even sure it existed?

Martin rode on, his mind filled with a marvelous vision. To please his mother—and to line his pockets—he would practice law for a few years. Then he would persuade his father that they should import some of those longhorns and try to interbreed them with Jerseys or Holsteins. Not all of them, though; some he would allow to breed their own kind. That bull with its spreading horns, its fierce gaze, had seemed to him evocative of another land—wilder, freer than this tidy England.

Two things blocked his dream. Midway of his last year at Oxford, his father had died. Soon bitter resentment was added to his grief. His mother, sole heir to his father's estate, sold the sheep farm to the first bidder and bought a house in a middle-class district of London. Martin didn't even know about it until just before spring vacation, when she came to tell him that the transaction was complete.

In answer to his outraged protests, she said, "I did it for you, my son." That was at least partly true, even though over the years she had grown to dislike the farm intensely. "As a member of the bar, you'll need a place in town to live."

Martin never did practice law, because even before that visit of his mother to Oxford, the Crimean War had begun. Recruiters visited the campus, and Martin, like most of the graduating class, signed up. Martin's mother, although terrified at the prospect of his going to war, was determined that at least he would go in style. Through the payment of a sum of money, as well as through the influence of her well-connected relatives, she secured him a commission in the Light Cavalry Brigade. He spent a few months in training and then embarked with his regiment for the Crimea.

Martin was not among the worst sufferers in that most mishandled of wars. The worst sufferers were the common soldiers—Russians on one side, British and French on the other—who had been sent into battle ill trained, ill equipped, and even ill fed. During the winter months they died by the thousands of typhus and other diseases.

But if Martin escaped death by both bullet and disease, he did take part in the most spectacular lunacy of that war, the charge of the Light Brigade. On the orders of Lord Raglan, who had seen no active service for the previous thirty-five years, the regiment was sent charging straight at a line of Russian field guns. As he thundered ahead, Martin was struck in the left ankle by a rifle bullet, but did not even feel it. It was a second bullet, striking his right shoulder, that knocked him from the saddle and probably saved his life. He lay among other wounded while the rest hurtled on, only to be cut down by cannonballs from the Russian heavy guns.

In the hospital the doctors found that the shoulder wound was of little consequence. The bullet had passed cleanly through. Bones in his ankle, though, had been smashed, so that he would limp for the rest of his life.

Lying in that makeshift hospital near Sevastopol, Martin heard tales of war profiteers, and of incompetent men who had bought high military rank, and of lives thrown away in battle like so much trash, just as his own life had almost been.

More and more he thought of going to America and staying there. Oh, not that he thought that the United

States was any stranger to corruption and greed and cruelty. He knew about black slavery, and about the Indians who were being exterminated as the white man moved west. He knew that even those longhorns that interested him so had been bred in Mexico on land recently lost to its more powerful northern neighbor.

But he felt that he himself would be a better person on the other side of the Atlantic, free to work at what interested him most, rather than spend his entire life in courtrooms.

He left the hospital only a few days before the exhausted Allies signed a peace treaty with the even more exhausted Russians. Martin felt at loose ends. He had yet to stand for his bar examination. Even if he passed it, he would not be able to practice law immediately. First he would have serve out a clerkship at a minuscule salary. That dream—the dream of a new breed of cattle, his cattle, moving across vast plains beneath a blue western sky—seemed far away indeed.

Then he received a letter from an old Oxford professor of his. Since Martin had done well in all his undergraduate studies, would he consider tutoring for a while? If a number of students engaged him, he would make quite a lot of money.

Martin had liked Oxford. Afternoon light falling on swaths of newly mown grass between the gravel walks. The cooing of pigeons under centuries-old eaves. The thoughtful but serene faces of elderly professors who had spent most of their lives here, and the fresh young voices of youngsters who had arrived only the previous week.

Too, working as a tutor would postpone the day when he would first walk into a courtroom, black-gowned and white-wigged. Martin had a superstitious feeling that on the day he did that, his fate would be sealed. His dream of vast, moving herds would remain just that—a dream.

Despite his mother's protests he returned to Oxford. In a small room up under the eaves of a building constructed four centuries before, he received his students. From the first there were quite a few of them. Paradoxically, his lame leg helped. Boys too young to have participated in the recent carnage liked to boast that their tutor had been part of the charge of the Light Brigade, the reckless but heroic action that Tennyson recently had enshrined in a poem.

The pupil who most aroused Martin's curiousity was older than the others, having entered Oxford when he was almost twenty. The story was that some very rich old woman, the widow of a textile manufacturer, was financing his education.

At their first interview, when Martin asked in which subjects he needed help, Jonathan Burke had answered, "All of them."

"Let me amend the question. Which is your strongest subject?"

Jonathan smiled. "The ladies. If you are clever in *that* subject, Mr. Cramer, you don't have to worry about the others."

Now Lady Athaire rose from her place at one end of the table. "Good night, gentlemen. I think I'll go upstairs now."

Of Jonathan her eyes asked, "Will you join me soon?" and his answered, "Of course."

A few minutes after his wife had left them, Sir Rodney pushed his brandy glass aside. "G'night, gennelmen." Leaning heavily on his footman's arm, he left the room.

Jonathan drained the last of his brandy, smiled at Martin, and said, "I think I'll join her ladyship for some cards. I feel uncommonly lucky tonight."

For a while Martin sat alone at the table, slowly turning the stem of his glass. Then he too went out the wide doorway and down the hall to his rooms.

15

Maryann did not report for her duties until mid-morning the next day. The housemaid who brought Maryann's breakfast, a very young, very plain girl with a thick Yorkshire accent, said that Lady Athaire did not want to see her until ten.

When Maryann entered her employer's room, she found her still in bed. Her bed jacket was of green satin. Her red hair hung in waves around her shoulders.

"Good morning, Lady Athaire." Then, hesitantly: "Are you ill?"

"Heavens, no!" And indeed, her lightly rouged and powdered face did appear to be in blooming health. "It's just that I'm feeling a bit lazy. Now, I've had the little desk brought from my sitting room to the corner over there. But first get paper and pencil and sit beside me. I'll tell you what I want you to write."

When Maryann was sitting beside the bed, pencil poised,

Elaine Athaire said, "First we must answer a letter from the Contessa della Ciobbotti."

After Lady Athaire spelled out the name for her, Maryann asked, "And the address?"

"Castle della Espigia, Monte Carlo."

She spoke with more than a little satisfaction. Who could have dreamed that Elaine Blodgett, living with her parents in two rooms above a dyer's shop, would someday correspond with contessas?

"What is it you want to say to her?"

"Well, of course I want to say something in answer to her letter. Now if I can just remember—"

She brightened. "Oh, yes. She said that she had been to Paris, where she had attended an Imperial Ball at the Tuileries, and where the Empress Eugenie seemed to single her out for special attention."

Maryann waited. When her employer remained silent, Maryann asked, "What else do you want to say?"

"Oh, the usual sort of thing. Something about the weather, and about the country being dull, and that I do look forward to going up to London for the season. But be sure to tell her that we went to quite a small party at Harrowstead House recently. The Prince of Wales was there, and the Duchess of Dorring, and the Marquis of Ware." It had in reality been an enormous crush, with even a a few people in trade in attendance, such as railroad millionaires. But it was unlikely that the Contessa would know that. Except for an occasional foray to Paris or London, she lived quite a secluded life.

"And make it quite short, Mrs. Fallon. After all, I have to copy it."

103

Maryann returned to the frail Louis Quinze desk, wrote rapidly for a few moments, paused for thought, wrote again. Finally she returned to the chair beside the bed.

"You've finished already?" Lady Athaire's voice was heavy with suspicion that anyone could write anything acceptable in that short a time.

"Yes. I do hope it's satisfactory. Shall I read it to you?" Lady Athaire nodded.

Maryann read:

"My dear Contessa,

How delightful to receive your letter. And how exciting to hear that in Paris you were a guest at the palace. But you seem surprised that the Empress singled you out for special attention. You are far too modest, my friend. Of course she would find interest in someone as charming as yourself.

The weather here is pleasant, but I do find the country dull. How I long for the London season.

Oh, I almost forgot. Recently I did have some respite from the rural dullness. My husband and I attended a rather small but brilliant party at Harrowstead House. The Prince of Wales was there, and the Dutchess of Dorring, and the Marquis of Ware.

I shall write no more at the moment, my dear friend. For one thing, as I have said, life is dull at Windmere, and for another, I have a touch of *la grippe*. But believe me, I remain,

Your devoted friend,
Elaine Athaire."

Lady Athaire beamed. "It's perfect, except that I've thought of a few more names to add to that part about

Harrowstead House. Now, I'd like you to write almost the same letter to Lady Anne Wharton, Cadogan Square, London, only don't say anything about the Tuileries Ball, of course. Instead, say that I hope her daughter's health has improved. And after that. . . .

Maryann scribbled rapidly, recording the names and addresses of the Countess of this and the Baroness of that, and of a Mrs. Custer in Bath. (How, Maryann wondered, did *she* get on the list?)

"Those will be enough letters for now. Just write them out. But first, bring me my lap desk—you'll find it folded up in that cupboard over there—and pen and ink, and my letter paper from the desk drawer."

Maryann settled the lap desk on the bed. As she placed a sheaf of Lady Athaire's writing paper on the desk, she noticed that the pages bore a large blue butterfly in one corner.

"You must be very fond of butterflies."

"I have been all my life."

As Elaine spoke, she had a memory dating from her sixth year. She had gone with her parents to a small pond on the moors where working-class families often gathered for picnics. Slipping away from the group, Elaine had wandered across the moor. It was then that she had seen her first butterfly, or at least the first she could remember. It clung to a stalk of heather, its brilliant blue wings opening and closing slowly. To the child it seemed infinitely precious and desirable. She ran to capture it. It flitted away, settled on another bit of heather, again flew away from her reaching hand.

She was still pursuing it when she topped a small rise.

She halted. Below her sat a plain young woman in a wicker cart drawn by a pony. A beautifully dressed blond girl of about Elaine's age stood near the cart, grasping a short pole with a netted scoop at its other end.

The magnificent winged creature settled onto a heather sprig a few yards from the blond child. "Oh, Miss Daisy!" the woman in the cart cried. "There is one! Get it, Miss Daisy, get it!"

The blond girl ran forward, swooped with the net, caught the struggling creature.

"I have it, Miss Smathers, I have it!"

"And so you do," the woman in the cart cooed. "What a clever young lady you are."

Her small heart filled with bitterness, Elaine watched the woman extract the iridescent creature from the net, pop it into a wooden box, place the box at her feet. That other little girl was rich. She had beautiful clothes, and a pony cart, and a woman to drive it, a woman who called her "Miss Daisy" in a honey-sweet voice. If you were rich, it was easy for you to make beautiful things your own.

If she were rich, she would have hundreds of butterflies, thousands.

Now, trying to use the flowing script she had been taught at finishing school, she began to copy Maryann's letter to the contessa.

Maryann was working on a third letter when a middle-aged maid in an elaborately fluted cap appeared in the doorway. Maryann realized that she must be Lady Athaire's personal maid—the one who, according to Sir Rodney during his first visit to the pig farm, couldn't "sew buttons on properly, or something like that."

106

"Your ladyship, Miss Olmstead is downstairs."

"Oh, dear! Well, I suppose I must see her. Have her sent up."

A few moments later a slender blond woman in her early twenties, with gray eyes set in an even-featured face, appeared in the doorway. Lady Athaire exclaimed, "My dear Diane! How kind of you to come to see me."

The blond young woman said, advancing toward the bed, "I had grown a bit anxious about you. I didn't see you at Lady Katherine's lawn party last Friday, and since I knew you must have been invited, I thought you might be ill."

"Oh, no. Please sit down, dear. As for Lady Katherine's party, Sir Rodney was feeling indisposed, and so at the last moment we decided against it." A certain falsity in her voice made Maryann think that the Athaires had not been invited. Furthermore, she felt that this Miss Olmstead knew it.

"But you are sure that *you* are all right, Lady Athaire? I thought you might have stayed out too late one of these long summer evenings and caught rheumatism from the damp. My mother does that sometimes."

After a moment her hostess laughed. "But your mother and I are scarcely of an age, dear."

"Oh, Lady Athaire! I didn't mean to imply that you were," she said in a tone that made it clear that she had meant to imply exactly that.

Lady Athaire said, as if the other woman hadn't spoken, "I feel a bit indolent, and so I decided to spend the morning dictating to my secretary." She raised her voice slightly. "Mrs. Fallon."

Maryann stood up, turned toward the two women. "This

107

is Miss Olmstead," Elaine Athaire said. "This is Mrs. Fallon, my secretary."

The blond head nodded. Maryann said, "How do you do, Miss Olmstead," and sat down and went back to work.

She was only vaguely aware of the talk of the two women behind her, something about an engagement announced in the *Times*. But even though she was absorbed in adding names to the first letter she had composed for Lady Athaire, she was aware of the hostility in the room. What had caused it? Why should they dislike each other so, these two women disparate in age and class? (Although the younger one was a plain Miss and the elder had a title, Maryann sensed that the younger's social origins were much higher.)

The maid again appeared in the doorway. "Mr. Burke would like to see you, if it pleases your ladyship."

Although she did not turn around, Maryann could sense that her employer was not at all pleased. "Very well. Have him come in."

He must already have been in the sitting room, because his wide shoulders filled the doorway almost as soon as the maid left it. He said, walking toward the bed, "What a pleasant surprise! *Two* lovely ladies. How are you, Diane?"

The young woman's voice suddenly sounded self-conscious, almost constricted. "Very well. And you are looking splendid, Jonathan."

Maryann wondered, Could *that* be it? Was Jonathan Burke the prize both women wanted?

He said, "I just came to pay my respects, Lady Athaire, and to see if that London jeweler has returned the bracelet I took to him for mending."

From the way they looked at each other, a stranger might never have guessed that he had spent three hours in this

108

room the night before. During the first two he had won fifteen pounds and eight shillings from Lady Athaire. During the last hour, in the wide bed, he had, as always, convinced her that he was well worth it.

She said, "Yes, the bracelet arrived by yesterday's post. He mended it beautifully."

Diane Olmstead said, still in that self-conscious tone, "Shall we see you at Lanford Manor next week, Mr. Burke? The young entry will be held, you know."

Maryann knew vaguely that "the young entry" was a fox-hunting term. Then she recalled from her reading of Thackeray and other English novelists that it referred to the first field trials of young foxhounds.

"Yes, I hope to be."

"What a pity that you don't ride, Lady Athaire!"

How Elaine Athaire longed to strike that falsely sympathetic young face. It was not *her* fault that she had not been taught to ride almost from infancy, as upper-class children of both sexes were. By the time her newly rich father got around to hiring a riding master for her, she had developed a fear and dislike of horses that she could not overcome.

Now she said, "Yes, it is a pity. I would love to ride. But if I get very close to horses, they have this terrible effect upon me. I start sneezing, and then I break out in spots." She paused and then addressed Jonathan. "Didn't I hear Martin Cramer mention at dinner last night that you and he were to meet at the Merson farm at one today? It was something about renewing some roofs there."

In Jonathan's memory there had been no such conversation. Nevertheless he said, "I do believe you are right."

"You know how tiresome he can be about promptness."

She looked at the ornate porcelain clock, all coy shepherdesses and piping shepherds, on the mantelpiece. "And it is already almost noon."

"You are right. I must be off." He kissed Miss Olmstead's hand and then Lady Athaire's, afterward holding the older woman's hand in his for a noticeable few seconds. "Good day, ladies."

On his way out he paused beside Maryann's desk. "Is everything going well, Mrs. Fallon?"

She looked up. Her beloved's face. Donald's blue eyes and warm, wide smile. Oh, God! Pain, actual physical pain, seemed to grip her vitals.

She managed to nod.

Leaning almost imperceptibly closer, he lowered his voice. "I am glad. I hope you will be here a long, long time."

Her pain gave way to loathing and rage. How was it he could look so much like Donald, this man who was not worthy to buckle Donald's shoes? This evil, arrogant man who, not content with setting those two women across the room at each other's throats, was now trying to charm *her*.

She was aware that behind her Diane Olmstead and Elaine Athaire had resumed their falsely animated chatter. Maryann said in a low, thick voice, "Please go. You are interfering with my work."

For a moment she glimpsed genuine amazement in the brilliant eyes. Why, this little American woman didn't find him attractive! In fact, to judge by the look in the upturned eyes, she hated him. Why? What had he ever done to her?

And then he felt an emotion that he had never experienced before. Not love. He did not believe that there was such a thing; people just imagined it. But he did feel a sudden, particularized lust such as he had never known.

Usually his appetite for women was strong but not very discriminating. As far as their bodies were concerned, he might well have been, although he was not, the man who originated the statement, "When the candles are out, all cats are gray." It was other qualities that made him prefer one woman to another—her money, her social standing, her intelligence—or rather, her lack of intelligence. Gullible women were easier to manage.

And yet here she was, this—this upper servant, this American woman with no money and, he sensed, too many brains. She was no good at all for any purpose of his. And yet he wanted her as he had never wanted another woman. Not just her body. He wanted to dominate her emotionally. He wanted to see in her eyes the same dazzled look he had seen in the eyes of other women.

But he could not proceed with her as he had with the others, whether peeresses or scullery maids. He would have to move slowly, politely, carefully.

"I'm very sorry, Mrs. Fallon. I didn't realize. A good day to you."

16

Shortly after noon, Diane Olmstead descended the steps to a waiting landau. She was aware that her legs trembled slightly with angry disappointment. She had hoped to encounter Jonathan in the hallway on her way out. But apparently he had gone off someplace, perhaps to that appointment Elaine Athaire had mentioned, although Diane's impression had been that the appointment was something her ladyship had made up on the spot.

As the landau with its smartly liveried driver carried her over the graveled drive toward the road, Diane reflected how absurd it was that she and Elaine should be rivals for a man. Diane seemingly had everything on her side. Youth. Beauty—not the showy prettiness that had caught Sir Rodney's eye but the cool, chiseled beauty that people called patrician. As for social standing, any comparison was laughable. Elaine tried to disguise her origins, but everyone knew about the dyer's shop and the formula that had brought sudden wealth. Diane, on the other hand, was the Honorable Diane Olmstead, third child and only daughter of Viscount Olmstead. And the viscount was rich, far richer than Sir Rodney Athaire.

Yes, there was no doubt in Diane's mind that, except for one cold fact, Jonathan would have been only too happy to marry her. Except for it, he would gladly have turned his back—at least for a while—on all other women, including Elaine. But the fact was there. If she married Jonathan, her father would cut her off without a penny. And Jonathan would never throw himself away on a penniless bride.

And so, she reflected bitterly, she would just have to stand by while Lady Athaire's aging husband gradually succumbed to his dissipations. It was highly probable that Jonathan would marry the wealthy widow.

Too absorbed in her unhappy musings to enjoy the beauty of the day—the hawthorn hedges loud with birdsong, the cloudless sky—she wished fleetingly that she could bring herself to accept some relationship with Jonathan other than marriage. But viscounts' daughters, after all, did not surrender their virginity in unhallowed beds.

She would just have to hope that she could persuade her father to give her both her heart's desire and her share of his vast inheritance. One thing heartened her a little. She knew that she, rather than any of her brothers, was her father's favorite.

There was another hope, so faint and so fantastic that just the thought of it brought a wry smile to her lips. She had heard rumors that Jonathan was not the natural child of his parents. He did not resemble them much, the story

113

went. Although light-complected, they were both short, and neither of them possessed Jonathan's comeliness or easy charm. At times she allowed herself to daydream that someday it would be discovered that Jonathan had been an infant of lofty lineage, somehow abandoned at the roadside, and found by a humble couple. . . .

But that, she knew, was on a level with those fairy stories about princelings abandoned in the forest, where they were found and raised by kindly woodcutters.

Oh, it was true that children were abandoned along the roads, some by couples too poor to feed yet another child, more often by unmarried girls who felt that it was their best or only recourse. Such children usually were rescued before starvation overtook them and were placed with families or in institutions. But it was hard to imagine a wellborn infant in such a situation.

No, Jonathan was no princeling. In a part of her mind not wholly given up to her infatuation, she also knew that he was not a man she or any other woman should marry. But she wanted him. She feared that she would want him her whole life through.

The carriage topped a rise. There below stood the Olmstead house, Clarmondly. Gray-stoned and many-turreted, it dated back to the time of Henry VII. Even the newer parts were two centuries older than the house she had just left.

Suddenly she remembered a story about a beloved daughter of the first Viscount Olmstead. The girl had eloped with a minstrel boy. Her father and a company of his men had pursued and found them and had riddled the boy with arrows until he fell lifeless at her feet. Then the girl, in full

114

sight of her doting father, had taken a dagger from her belt and stabbed herself to death.

Was she a throwback to that wild-hearted girl? Although her appearance and deportment at her presentation had won the approval of the rather prudish occupant of Buckingham Palace, Diane feared that in her heart she was more like her remote ancestress than she wanted to admit.

17

By teatime, when Lady Athaire dismissed her for the day, Maryann felt exhausted. She had composed eight letters. As the day wore on, her employer had become more exacting. Maryann had had to revise one letter—to a certain Lady Langford—three times before Elaine Athaire pronounced it satisfactory. Also, there had been the matter of a bill for a pair of white kidskin gloves. Although the morning's post had brought a bill from the glovemaker, Lady Athaire maintained that the gloves had been paid for and insisted that her employee search through the desk and dressing-table drawers and other receptacles for the receipted bill. Somewhat to her surprise, Maryann found that Lady Athaire had been correct. The receipt lay in a drawer of a small jewel chest.

In addition to all that, Pompom had escaped twice into the corridor. Both times Maryann had pursued him. Once aided by the personal maid and once by a footman, she had eventually caught him and returned him, narrow-eyed and with ears laid back, to his adoring owner.

Consequently, Maryann was glad to go to her own shabby rooms at the end of the day. Someone had brought a pot of tea and placed it on a spirit lamp. Gratefully she drank the hot liquid and ate the small sweet biscuit that accompanied it. Later, the same maid who had served her the night before brought her a small chicken pot pie.

As the long summer twilight faded into night, she felt both tired and restless. Longingly she thought of her father's library in the parsonage and of the much smaller collection of books she and Donald had kept at the farm. She had brought none of them with her. A third-class passenger, crowded with two other women into a small cabin, could bring only the most limited amount of baggage. At her sister-in-law's farm she had always been so tired by the time she fell into her narrow bed that the thought of reading had seldom crossed her mind. But now, when her exhaustion was more nervous than physical, she longed for the distraction of a book.

There was a library in this house.

Surely no one would object if she borrowed a book. After all, she would not have been hired as Lady Athaire's secretary if she were not reasonably literate.

She turned on the gas jets, and standing before the rather wavy mirror above her washstand, she smoothed her hair. Then she went down the front staircase, meeting no one, although on the floor below she did catch a glimpse of a footman, a filled coal scuttle in one hand, knocking on the door of a room. Sir Rodney's room? Probably. Younger persons would find the evening too warm for a fire.

She started to open the library's double doors and then hesitated. The big room's gas lights had been lit. Someone was in there. Then she told herself that that was no reason to stay out, since it probably was only her fellow employee, Martin Cramer. It was hard to imagine any other member of the household choosing to visit the library.

But she was wrong. Jonathan Burke stood across the room holding an opened book, a small one bound in faded brown leather. He turned his head, smiled at her, and said with automatic gallantry, "How very delightful!"

She stiffened. Be careful, he warned himself. Go very slowly. For some reason, this one was different from the others. He said, "What I meant was that it is good to know that someone else in this house is interested in books."

She gave a noncommittal nod. He returned to the shelf the book he had been reading. "Could I help you find something? I'm quite familiar with this room."

She said vaguely, "I'm not in a mood for anything too serious. Perhaps a novel—"

"Jane Austen? I am sure there is a set of her books here. Or have you read them all?"

"Every one. And yet I'm glad you mentioned her. I find I would love to read *Emma* again."

He crossed the room. Rolling a set of low library steps close to the shelves, he climbed to the top one and then came back to her with a book in his hand. "*Emma.*"

"Thank you." Was his suggestion of Jane Austen just happenstance, or was he clever at judging other people's tastes?

She hesitated and then said, "Mr. Burke, would you mind telling me where you were born?"

118

For a moment he wondered how she would react if he said, "I have no idea." Instead he said, "In a little town about ten miles from York. My people were shopkeepers. Greengrocers, to be exact."

He thought of that pair, Toby and Adeline Burke. Even as a boy of seven, he had felt that they were alien to him. By the time he was nine, he had felt superior to them. He could make them believe anything, that the sixpence they had given him to buy a pencil box for school had not been spent on sweets but had slipped through a hole in his pocket. That it was not *he* who had suggested shaving elderly Mrs. Tubbs's even more elderly collie and covering the animal with tar and chicken feathers. That in fact he'd tried to stop the other boys from doing it.

A few days after his tenth birthday, he had had the extreme good fortune of being almost run down by a carriage in front of his parents' shop.

The sole passenger in the carriage was its owner, Mrs. Samuel Gaitsby, the extremely rich widow of a textile manufacturer. She ordered her driver to halt, then to go back and get the boy and bring him to her so that she could be sure he was all right.

He had lifted his beautiful eyes, his seraphic face, toward the befeathered and bejeweled woman in the carriage and had assured her he was right fine, ma'am, except for a bit of a twist he'd given his ankle getting out of the way. Where did he live? At the greengrocers' shop, just over there.

The next week Mrs. Gaitsby had returned, "just to be sure the little lad is all right." The Burkes, awed but delighted, invited her into their seldom-used parlor and served her tea. Jonathan stood close to her, his angelic face wor-

119

shipful. He smiled his melting smile whenever he caught her eye.

The first of his feminine conquests, Mrs. Gaitsby was also among the most vulnerable. It was not surprising that she was already thinking of him as the grandson she had never had nor was likely to have. Her son and only child was now middle-aged, unmarried, and seemed determined to remain so. Since he preferred to spend most of his time traveling in Europe and the Middle East, his mother had not even seen him for several years.

Not long after taking tea in the Burkes' parlor, Mrs. Gaitsby proposed to them that Jonathan leave the village school and attend a nearby boarding school at her expense. Still later, she managed to get him into Winchester. If his lingering Yorkshire accent brought him ridicule—and it did—his prowess on the playing fields brought him admiring respect.

After Winchester, Mrs. Gaitsby sent him to Oxford. There it was the same story. His origins caused scornful amusement in some, but for others his extreme good looks, athletic abilities, and clever although somewhat lazy mind outweighed his handicaps. And when he chose to become a member of a group that dabbled in the occult—some for amusement's sake, some seriously—he found himself dining and drinking with youths whose surnames were among the oldest and most honored in the kingdom.

The Burkes never visited him at either Winchester or Oxford, and from his sixteenth year onward he returned to the greengrocers' shop not more than once or twice a year. But he never neglected his patroness, Mrs. Gaitsby. During the college term, he tried to spend part of every week-end with her at her London home, and during the long holidays he was an almost permanent guest at her country place near Northampton.

He treated her with gallantry that brought color to her faded cheeks. Now and then he whispered indiscretions into her ear that caused her to strike him with her folded fan, like some beauty of the previous century. When it was all over, he reflected that he had really earned the emerald cufflinks she had given him, and the ruby ring, and the monthly allowance from which, despite his extravagant tastes in food, clothing, and entertainment, he had been able to save a good sum.

But in the end he had missed the big prize. Knowing that the estate was not entailed, he had expected to be named Mrs. Gaitsby's heir. Unfortunately, a few months before her death, her wandering son came back. He was engaged, he said, and showed her a picture of his betrothed, a demure-looking young woman in her midtwenties. Mrs. Gaitsby changed her will, leaving five hundred pounds to her "dear young friend and protégé, Jonathan Burke," and everything else to her son.

But it did not matter too much, because by then, at a party given by Mrs. Gaitsby's country neighbors, Jonathan had met a certain Lady Athaire, wife of a rich, hard-drinking husband considerably older than herself.

And so he was quite sincere when he had said to Martin Cramer, the ex-calvaryman-turned-tutor whom he had engaged to pull him through his last year at Oxford, "My best subject is the ladies. If you are good at that, you don't need to be good at anything else."

Now Maryann Fallon asked, riffling through the pages

of *Emma*, "Have you been back to see your parents recently?"

"Not as often as I should," he said with an engaging air of frankness. "This place is a big responsibility, and then —well, I'm afraid I am not as dutiful a son as I should be."

As a matter of fact, he had not been back to the green-grocers' shop for two years. It was then that he had become certain that what he had suspected all along was true. The Burkes were not his natural parents.

He looked down at Maryann Fallon. Damn this girl with the beautiful, kissable mouth and the eyes that seemed to be trying to look right through him. She did not like him. She distrusted him. Why? He didn't know. All he knew was that she was going to end up adoring him, reaching out feverishly for him. He was absolutely determined about that.

But as he had told himself that afternoon, he would have to go very slowly with her.

He said, "Why don't you look around and see what books are here? Most of them seem inexpressibly dreary, but you might find something of interest. Well, I must bid you good night. I'm to ride out with my assistant again early in the morning."

When he had gone, Maryann walked across the room and scanned a shelf at about shoulder height. Yes, there it was, the small book bound in worn brown leather. She took it down.

The title on the spine was one word: *Zadkiel.* She opened the book. It was in Latin. The Latin she had learned at the academy had grown rusty, so much so that she could read only a phrase here and there. Nevertheless, the word *Zad-*

kiel awoke some echo in her memory. Somehow it was connected with her father. Something in one of his sermons? A character in a story he had told her when she was a child? She could not remember.

She replaced the worn book. Then, clutching *Emma*, she left the library.

18

Jonathan Burke stood by the window of his darkened bedroom, looking out. It was a large room, and sumptuous, its fireplace manteled with white marble, its mahogany furniture upholstered in dark blue velvet that matched the draperies. Until Jonathan's advent here, this room had been reserved for the most distinguished of visitors to Windmere.

The moon, three nights from full, was up now. Silvery radiance flooded the garden paths between the clumps of rose bushes. Three nights from now, he would be meeting with some of his old Oxford friends. The Honorable Averil and Honorable Arthur Makelin, twin sons of the Earl of Clathby. Young Lord Walter Marly, and several other untitled but wellborn young men, as well as a few rich merchants' sons.

For Jonathan, joining that group had at first been only a way of associating himself with young men who, no matter what their eccentricities, had been born into the privileged classes. How many of them took the group seriously he did not know.

He did know one thing. Since joining the group he had enjoyed good fortune. True, he had missed out on the millions he had hoped to inherit from old Mrs. Gaitsby. But that didn't matter too much because by then he had won Elaine Athaire as a consolation prize. Elaine would never be as rich as Mrs. Gaitsby had been. But she was a generation younger and really still quite attractive. Also, as she managed to convey to him soon after they met, her husband's estate was not entailed upon their only son, who was then in his first year at Eton. In fact, when Sir Rodney had first fallen in love with Elaine Blodgett, he had apparently feared that neither his appearance nor his title would induce such a dazzling creature to marry him. And so he had promised to draw up a will to ensure that she would be his sole heir, no matter how many children they might have.

Within a couple of years after becoming Elaine Athaire's lover, Jonathan had had another bit of good fortune. Sir Rodney, Elaine told Jonathan, was going to have to pension off his aged estate manager. If Jonathan wanted the position, she was sure he could have it.

Jonathan jumped at the chance. Two years earlier, he had managed to get through Oxford, without honors but with a degree. Since then he had been idling away his time in the town of Oxford, living in rather cheap rooms off the five hundred pounds Mrs. Gaitsby had left him. And now here was a chance to live in a house where he had felt privileged just to be a frequent guest.

At her suggestion, he went up to Windmere immediately to be interviewed by Sir Rodney. Within minutes, Sir Rodney had told him that the position was his. Jonathan couldn't be sure why the old boy was so obliging. Surely he knew he was hiring his wife's lover. Perhaps he feared Elaine's temper, which could be as fiery as her hair. Or perhaps he just did not care who managed the estate, as long as he was left free to indulge himself in drink, tussles with housemaids, and whatever other amusements appealed to him.

The first thing Jonathan did after being installed at Windmere was to spend several hours in the room that had served his predecessor as an office. He went through papers pertaining to the estate until he found what he was looking for—a copy of Sir Rodney's will. Just as Elaine had said, it left everything to her.

But he also discovered during his first few days at Windmere that the position involved far more work than he had realized. It was not just a matter of keeping an account of rents received and monies dispersed. His predecessor had kept records of almost daily trips to tenant farms, where he had inspected diseased cattle, leaky barn roofs, and blighted apple trees. Neither his excellent salary nor his splendid rooms could reconcile Jonathan to a life spent inspecting infected cow udders and moldy haystacks.

It was then that he thought of Martin Cramer, that tutor who had pulled him through his final year at Oxford. Not only had Martin been quite frank about his farm background. He had also talked of a certain bee in his bonnet, something about creating a new breed of cattle. Might Martin be interested in acting as steward here in return for, say, half of the salary Sir Rodney paid? Jonathan would not mind giving up that much. He already had seen ways in which, by altering the account books, he would be able to pocket a few pounds here and a few pounds there. Besides, he and Elaine often played cards, and poor Elaine's luck was phenomenally bad.

He proposed to Elaine the idea of bringing in an assistant. She was delighted by the idea because it would mean that Jonathan could spend more time with her. As for Sir Rodney, he merely shrugged. As long as he would not be paying out a second salary, why should he mind?

Jonathan knew that Martin Cramer was still tutoring at Oxford. He wrote to him and received a prompt and favorable reply

The arrangement had worked beautifully. Jonathan had plenty of leisure time. And Martin, peculiar fellow that he was, loved his job. He had even managed to breed two of a tenant farmer's Jerseys to a strange kind of bull imported from a place in America with a peculiar name. Oh, yes. Texas. The results, a bull calf and twin heifers, had been born last spring. Jonathan had not seen them yet, but Martin visited them every few days.

Jonathan yawned. Thank heaven Elaine had not wanted to see him tonight. Tired out, he looked forward to eight or nine hours of sleep in his own bed. He took one last look at the moonlight-silvered garden. Then he lit one of the gas jets, drew the draperies, and began a leisurely undressing.

19

Maryann's second day in Lady Athaire's employ was much easier. Pompom escaped into the corridor only once. The post brought no bills at all and only two letters that Lady Athaire felt should be answered immediately. Maryann spent most of the day reading aloud to her employer from the Court Calendar in the *Times* and from *Wycherly's Weekly*, one of several papers devoted to the more indiscreet doings of the upper classes.

When she finished her solitary supper, Maryann still felt full of unused energy. For a while she looked down into the garden, spectral in the glow of cloud-diffused moonlight. After that she read two more chapters of *Emma*. Then she decided to take a walk up the road, at least as far as that abbey "Old Harry's" men had wrecked.

With a dark shawl over her head to ward off the evening dew, she went down the back stairs and out onto the garden terrace. Then she circled the house to the drive. Light shone through a crack in the draperies of what she knew was the dining room. Perhaps the Athaires and their steward and his assistant were still at table, although that seemed unlikely since it was almost ten o'clock. More likely, tired servants were setting the room to rights and laying the fire for the morning before they crept to their third-floor rooms.

She went down the graveled drive and turned left onto the dirt road. The cloud cover was thick enough that no area of the sky seemed especially luminous. Instead, the moonlight was so diffused that the light seemed that of early dawn rather than premidnight. The road looked pale gray. Later on, so did some sheep feeding in a meadow beyond a low stone wall. She could see the ruined abbey, dark on its hilltop, with gray light filling pointed arches that once, more than likely, had held stained glass.

Someone was coming toward her down the road. A man. He was above medium height and rather thin, with his dark head bare to the night. As he drew closer, she noticed that he limped slightly. Martin Cramer then, the assistant steward.

When they were a few feet apart, she said, "Good evening, Mr. Cramer."

He halted. "What do you think you are doing, wandering along the road this time of night?"

Irked by his almost harsh tone, she said, "I am not wandering. I am walking, just as you are."

"I am a man. That makes everything different."

"In what way?"

He had an impulse to tell her, in words of one syllable. But the truth was that she was not in much danger and probably would not be even if she walked this road two nights from now. Surely Jonathan Burke and those high-born idiots he ran with would have sense enough not to trifle with a young woman like this—spirited, articulate, and a protégé of Sir Rodney Athaire's. They usually chose their victims from among those too young or humbly born to dare to protest—or from those already too dissolute to even want to.

Just the same, she would be wiser not to wander about by herself at night. He told her so.

She said, "I'm not afraid."

"You have grown extraordinarily courageous in a very short time. Just the day before yesterday, you were frightened out of your wits by a simpleton wearing a mask."

"How could I know what she was? She appeared to be some sort of—monstrous dwarf. Anyway, I was startled rather than frightened."

"You looked more than startled when I picked you up off the path."

"All right! I thanked you for your services at the time. I thank you again now. And so will you let me proceed? I plan to walk up to that old abbey."

"Please!" He reached out and caught her arm. "It is dangerous up there at night."

She looked up at him. Through the material of her dress she could feel the warmth of his hand on her arm. For just a moment, something stirred in her, something she thought had died forever one icy December morning. Then she drew her arm away.

"Dangerous?"

"There are loose stones about. You might stumble."

"I'll be careful. Besides, the light is quite good." She moved past him.

"Mrs. Fallon."

He did not touch her this time, but his voice was so urgent that she stopped and faced him.

"Please do not go up to the abbey." There might be a few of them up there, making God only knew what preparations for their silly "services." If they thought she was spying on them, things might get ugly. They might not hesitate long enough to realize that she was not just some farmer's wife or daughter.

He went on. "The—the place does not have a good reputation. Vagabonds often take shelter there."

She realized that might be true. English roads were not as dangerous as they had been during those times she had read about, when highwaymen robbed and killed people, even those traveling in groups. But England still had many desperately poor people. Else why should they send their girl children down into the mines, or even go down there themselves? And of course there must be thousands of others who were too old or sick—or too rebellious—to go into the mines or textile mills. Probably it was men of that sort who roamed the roads and took refuge in places like that old abbey.

"Please, Mrs. Fallon. Come back to the house with me." He smiled. It was the first time she had seen him smile. It did attractive things to his face. "You don't want me to lose sleep worrying about you, do you? I must make a round of the tenant farms tomorrow, and I will need an early start."

131

"Very well, Mr. Cramer. I would not dream of cheating you of your sleep."

For a while they walked in silence back toward Windmere. Then he asked, "Have you been a widow for long, Mrs. Fallon?"

She thought, Since about three minutes of eight in the morning, last December fifth. Aloud she said, "A little more than six months."

"You and your husband had no children?"

"A little boy. He's three years old now." Her heart twisted. She thought of his stretching out chubby arms the day of her departure, his small face filled with terror and outrage and disbelief.

"You must miss him."

"Dreadfully. I hope to be able to send for him soon. Now that I have well-paid work, I will be able to save money." She checked herself. No point in chattering on about her personal affairs.

"You plan to raise him in England?"

"Yes. You see, eventually he and I will have a small inheritance—one half of the farm owned by my husband's parents."

"I was a farmer's son."

"Sheep farming?"

"Mostly, but some cattle. I'd still be there if my mother had not sold the land." He paused. "I should think you would want to return to America if it is at all possible. It must be a wonderful place to raise a child."

She shrugged. "New England and Old England aren't so different. The same sort of beauty—meadows and meandering rivers and low hills. And except that New England

132

has no mines, there are the same cruel alternatives for the poor, especially the female poor—long, long hours as a servant, often dangerous labor in the textile mills, or, when you get old, the bread of charity in some poor farm."

"I was thinking of the western part of the United States. Texas, say."

"You've been there?"

"No, but I plan to go someday." He hesitated and then began to talk of the bull with the long horns, and the two Jerseys bred to him, and the three calves that had been produced. He spoke of his dream of vast herds of cattle drifting across a plain, cattle with the hardiness of Mexican longhorns and the meat- and milk-producing capacities of long-established breeds.

Then he fell abruptly silent. He seldom talked to anyone of his plans. Why should he tell this woman, who despite her demure appearance was one of Sir Rodney's trollops? Different from the others in looks and manners and far more expensive—thirty pounds a year—but still one of his trollops.

They moved in silence down Windmere's graveled drive. Then Maryann asked, "Would you mind a personal question?"

His voice was cold. "Probably not."

"Why is it that you limp?"

"An old bullet wound. I was in the Crimean War."

He did not mention the charge. Because so much had been said and written about that idiotic episode, he almost never mentioned it to anyone. And certainly he was not going to discuss it with this woman.

Maryann was aware of his coldness, and of the reason

for it. But what could she do about it? Could she say, "I have no intention of accommodating Sir Rodney. He has not approached me yet, but if he does, I will make that clear. If he decides then that he wants to dispense with my services to his wife, let him do so."

To answer an accusation that Martin Cramer had not actually made would make her appear undignified, cheap.

She remained silent until they reached the first of the semicircular steps. Then she said, "Good night. I am going around to the garden entrance."

He did not offer to accompany her. "Good night."

The garden still appeared strange in that diffused light. Everything was washed with gray except the luminous reflecting balls on their pedestals. She mounted steps, crossed the flagstoned terrace, opened the door. A young footman with rough dark hair, evidently posted there to guard the rear entrance during late night and early morning hours, sat slumped in a straight chair beneath a flickering gas jet, sound asleep.

Quietly Maryann climbed the stairs. On the next, or family, floor, she glanced down the wide corridor with its candle sconces affixed to paneled walls. Most of those expensive, scented tapers had been extinguished, leaving wide stretches of darkness between pools of dim light. She climbed to the servants' floor, where one hallway gas jet burned. She walked toward her room. At the other end of the hall someone emerged from a room, closed its door, turned toward her.

It was Sir Rodney. They halted a few feet from each other. She saw that he looked not only embarrassed but disgruntled. She could not tell whether his ill temper arose just from being caught on the servants' floor or from some other cause as well.

She said, trying to speak in a normal voice, "Good evening, Sir Rodney."

His bald head nodded an acknowledgment.

"Or rather, good night," she said, and started to move past him to go to her door.

"Wait. I have something to say to you."

She stood still, hoping that a pleasant but firm expression would discourage him from any amorous notions he might be entertaining.

The housemaid he had just left, a new addition to the staff, had doused herself with cheap scent in anticipation of his visit. The scent, combined with the smell of grease —she'd had to help out in the kitchen that day—had been too much for him. He had said something about being "tired" and beat a retreat.

But now here, providentially, was this young American woman, a quite beautiful one even though he had never cared for slender brunettes. He was paying her salary, and a damned fine salary it was. Why couldn't he do what he had planned the day he hired her? Why couldn't he take her arm and say, "All right, my girl, let us go to your room. You and I are going to have a bit of frolic, whether you like it or not."

He knew why he could not do it. He was afraid. Afraid that even if he overpowered her, ripped those cheap black clothes off her, he would see in her eyes not just fear and repulsion. He would see scorn.

He always had been afraid of being scorned, even when he was a young boy. Scorned by his father, a hard-drinking,

hard-riding eighteenth-century-style peer who had re-
garded his son and heir as a mollycoddle. Scorned by his
schoolmates because he was fat and no good at games. And
he had been so afraid that Elaine, a dyer's daughter, would
scorn him that even before he proposed he had mentioned
that in his opinion a wife should always be her husband's
sole heir.

Maryann's voice broke the lengthening silence. "Yes, Sir
Rodney?"

She had sounded quite calm, but he could tell that she
had sensed his fear. "I have forgotten what I intended to
say. Penalty of growing older, I daresay. Anyway, it could
not have been important. Good night, Mrs. Fallon."

He walked toward the landing of the front stairs. Some
parcels from Paris had arrived this morning. Under lock
and key now, they were in that room that no one but himself
ever entered. Perhaps it would cheer him to open his parcels. But no. He felt too dispirited even to look at his new
things, let alone try them on.

He descended the rest of the flight of stairs, walked to
the suite of rooms opposite his wife's, and went inside.

20

It was the next day that Maryann discovered the quarry. Around two that afternoon her employer announced that she would like to take a nap. Glad of the respite, Maryann moved through the rose garden and then on out the gate in the tall rear hedge. She found herself in a grassy meadow, starred with daisies and surrounded by a low stone wall. Perhaps Athaire horses were pastured there at times, although no domestic animals at all were there at the moment. She maneuvered her skirts over the wall and then stopped for an indecisive moment on a footpath. If she turned left and climbed a low hill, she probably would see the ruined abbey. She decided to explore in the other direction.

She crossed open country where, among the purple heather, she occasionally saw wild roses and a flower that resembled the familiar wild geranium of the Connecticut woods. Then she climbed a low hill and circled around a spinney of beech trees. There below her, in its cup of similar hills, was the quarry. Its straight, steep sides were of the same gray stone as Windmere. Its sunken water was blue and still in the afternoon sunlight.

At its edge was a flat rectangular stone almost the size of a double bed. She walked within a few inches of its edge and then, bending at the waist, looked over. The sight of the sheer plunge to the dark blue water sent a shiver down her body.

She retreated a few steps, sat down, and turned her face, eyes closed, up to the sunlight. A twittering sound made her open them. In pursuit of tiny insects invisible to her, swallows were wheeling and diving above the quarry.

Watching the aerial ballet, she thought, How lovely and peaceful it is here. She heard the sound of a fish leaping from the water and then falling back. How did the fish get there? Had someone stocked the water with trout or bass? Or did some underground stream bring fish into the quarry?

She also wondered if young boys ever came there to climb down the rough-hewn steps she could see on the right-hand side of the quarry. Probably not often. In this far-from-affluent part of England young boys, when not in school, would be at work in the fields or behind shop counters.

The thought of work reminded her of her own duties. Lady Athaire might want her to write another letter or two before teatime. Reluctantly she got to her feet and turned toward Windmere.

She was about halfway there when, as she topped a slight rise, she saw a squat figure moving toward her. After a while she realized it was Luddy, wearing those same tattered garments, so dirty it was impossible to be sure of their original color. Today Luddy was minus a mask but wore daisies stuck in her tangled hair. Despite the daisies, she in no way resembled an Ophelia. Her seamed and yet childlike face grinning, she blocked Maryann's way.

She said, giving no sign that she realized that they had met before, "Spare me a tuppence, lady?"

"I'm sorry. I don't have any money with me."

Luddy's grin widened. "Not even tuppence. Happen that's why you're out here. Think you might meet a man with a bit o' brass in his breeches."

She added a suggestion so lewd that Maryann felt staggered.

"Well, good luck to you, luv." Luddy moved on toward the quarry.

Shocked yet amused, Maryann continued on her way.

It was the next night that she went to the abbey.

A full moon, floating in a cloudless sky, tempted her to make the journey. As she stood at her window, looking down at a garden path bleached almost snow-white by the light, she thought of how the abbey would appear tonight on its hilltop, its ruined arches black against the dark blue sky.

With her shawl over her head, she slipped down the back stairs. The footman-guard had not yet taken his place on the chair beneath the flaring gas jet. She went out the garden door, around the house. She hoped that she would not again encounter Martin Cramer. But if she did, she would tell him firmly that although she would follow his advice not to approach the abbey, she would not deny herself a walk on this lovely night.

She did not meet Martin Cramer. As she moved along

the moon-bleached road, it remained empty. After a moment she realized that she felt a certain disappointment that no slightly limping figure moved toward her. The discovery dismayed her. It was unthinkable that she, in only the seventh month of her widowhood, should feel drawn to any man, especially one who obviously considered her at best an adventuress and at worst little more than a harlot.

She went past a clump of beech trees and then turned a curve in the road. Now she could see the abbey on its rounded hilltop. She stopped short, puzzled. A flickering glow seemed to emanate from those arches that, before Old Harry's time, perhaps had framed stained-glass portraits of the Virgin and the saints. Was it a trick of the moonlight? Or had some of those vagabonds Martin had mentioned kindled a cooking fire? Surely it would do no harm for her to move close enough to determine the source of that flickering light.

Moving slowly, she walked a few yards down the road, stopped. Yes, there was the entrance to a narrow path that led upward through gorse and heather.

She climbed, her skirts pulled close about her to keep them from snagging on the bushes. Often a dip in the path made her lose sight of the abbey.

A tall, roughly columnar rock at the roadside ahead. Just an ordinary boulder? Or one of those standing stones that the mysterious early inhabitants of this island had erected for purposes unknown? She started toward it, halted. Somewhere a horse had nickered, and another had answered.

Horses? Vagrants would not have horses. But a band of gypsies almost certainly would.

Very cautious now, she went around the boulder, stopped short.

A tall figure in a hooded black robe stood a few yards away on the path. His face was turned away from her. Apparently he looked toward where those horses had nickered.

For a stunned instant she thought of the monks, dead these three hundred years, who had lived and worshiped in what was now a ruin. Then any thought that she was seeing a phantom vanished. Another explanation had come to her, in its way far more frightening.

She backed away around the rock, turned. Her feet soundless on the dirt path, she descended several yards. Yes, here it was, another path branching off to the left and apparently slanting upward. She took it, trying to move rapidly and yet with the least possible damage to her clothing.

She tried to remember, too, all that she had read about the Hellfire Club and similar organizations that had flourished for a time during the last century. Made up of rich and often titled young wastrels, they had terrorized both Londoners and people in the countryside, robbing, raping, vandalizing. And some of the clubs had believed—or pretended to believe—in Satanism. They had gathered in out-of-the-way places, preferably once-sanctified buildings, to celebrate the Black Mass. The naked young women placed on the altars at such ceremonies sometimes had been prostitutes, sometimes kidnapped young farm girls, drugged or terrorized into helplessness.

Were such clubs again in fashion among certain rich idlers? Had Jonathan Burke, raised as a greengrocer's son, ingratiated himself at Oxford by joining such a group, or perhaps even by assuming the leadership of it?

She had to find out, if she possibly could. She had

to know all that was knowable about him, this man who almost surely was her lost beloved's brother, her little boy's uncle.

The path, more meandering than the one she had left, led gradually upward. She saw no more sentinels. Evidently one lookout had been deemed sufficient to give an alarm if the local constabulary or a band of outraged country people appeared on the road below. And those were the kind of intruders they must feel they had to guard against, not a lone young woman stealing along the paths.

Now she could hear something else besides the occasional sibilance of her skirts against the bushes. From the hilltop ruin came a low chanting.

Around the abbey itself there was a cleared space. No concealing bushes—just grass, so tall that some blades curved over, with moonlight running like quick silver along them. She hesitated for a moment, then moved swiftly to the abbey's rough stone wall and flattened herself against it.

She waited. No break in the chanting, and no other sound. Still keeping close to the wall, she sidled to the edge of an archway, looked around it.

Moonlight poured into the roofless ruin to mingle with the light of candles. Candles on the ancient stone altar. Candles held by cowled figures who lined the abbey's center aisle, lighting the way for the four robed and hooded men who moved down it. They bore on their shoulders a litter draped with black satin. Her full-figured nakedness very white against the shiny material, a young blond woman lay on the litter. She was giggling. She raised her head, apparently to look at the men lining the aisle. Even from that distance and in that uncertain light, Maryann could see the blurred look in the girl's eyes. That dazed expression, plus the giggles, made her think that the girl on the litter was drunk or drugged.

Cowls hid the faces of all the men except one. Jonathan Burke stood behind the altar, his head flung back as he looked at the upside-down cross he held aloft. The four litter-carriers laid their burden on the altar.

Turning, Maryann plunged down the path between the bushes, too sickened to guard her clothing as carefully as before from the gorse thorns. She did not stop until she had almost reached the road. Then she moved off the path, dropped to the ground, and laid her cheek against her updrawn knees.

It was not just opportunism that had led Jonathan to that devil-worshiping cult. Some of the others might be play-acting. He was not. As he looked up at that inverted cross, that mockery of the crucified Christ, there was no trace of that charming smile of his. His face had been white with emotion, his upturned eyes filled with fervor.

He truly worshiped the devil.

And that, Maryann felt, meant that he was more than an evil man. He was an insane one.

Where had that madness come from? Had he inherited it from Ian Fallon? If so, it meant that the seeds of that madness might have lain dormant in her beloved Donald. It meant—unbearable thought!—that the seeds might unfold someday in her precious son.

She must learn of his origins, this man who was almost a mirror-image of the man she had married.

According to her arrangement with Lady Athaire, Maryann was to have a day off every two weeks. Her first such holiday was several days away, but when it came she would visit the people who had reared Jonathan Burke.

She was halfway back to Windmere along that moon-flooded road when she suddenly realized that even before this she should have guessed that Jonathan might be a Satanist. Her second night at Windmere, she had entered the library to find him reading a small book with the word *Zadkiel* on its ancient spine.

She could remember now that she had first seen that word when she was ten. It had been in an article her father was preparing for *The Theosophical Quarterly*. She had asked him what it meant, and he had answered that Zadkiel was another name for the Devil.

21

As it happened, Maryann was able to visit the Burkes earlier than she had expected to.

When she entered her employer's bedroom the next morning, Lady Athaire said, "Never mind the letters for a while." Dressed in a green muslin morning gown, she sat in a small armchair in front of her tilted petit-point frame. Ever since Maryann had been at Windmere, Lady Athaire had been working on a cover for a footstool. Its design was of blue butterflies hovering over lilies-of-the-valley. "Bring a chair over and sit beside me."

After Maryann obeyed, Lady Athaire lowered her voice, even though there was no one in either of the rooms. "I want you to go to the railroad station in Garwith tomorrow morning." Garwith was a small village two miles away. "There are several trains to York. I think the earliest leaves at seven-thirty. Anyway, Lothar will know. He will take you to the station."

145

"In York, you are to go straight to my jewelers, Hartwick and Sons. Tell them to give you that emerald necklace and earring set I looked at last month. I will need it for the ball Sir Rodney and I are giving about a fortnight from now."

Elaine knew that the jewelry made her green eyes look greener, her hair redder. A mirror in Hartwick's shop had told her so. And she would need to look her very best the night of the ball. Diane Olmstead would be there. And I will not, Elaine thought, I simply will *not* be outshone by that pasty-faced aristocrat.

Aloud she went on. "Mr. Hartwick not only will give you the jewelry. He will give you some banknotes to give to me. Now, this is strictly between the two of us. Do you understand?"

Bewildered, Maryann said, "I am afraid not. You are buying jewels from this Mr. Hartwick, and yet he will send *you* money?"

"I have an arrangement with him." Although her voice was still low, it had sharpened. "He will send a bill to my husband, or rather to that stiff-necked Martin Cramer. It will be for—somewhat more than the actual price of the jewelry."

Maryann understood then. This Hartwick would pay Lady Athaire in cash the difference between the actual price and the price listed on the bill. Thus she would have additional pounds to lose to Jonathan at cards or to squander on him in some other fashion.

"Don't look so shocked," Lady Athaire said. "It is done all the time. Lots of ladies have such arrangements with their jewelers and dressmakers and so on. And in my case I see no reason at all for feeling guilt. My husband often borrows money from my father."

Maryann said vaguely but agreeably, "Of course." Then: "But Lady Athaire! Such jewelry must be valuable. I do not like to take the responsibility—"

"Nonsense, my girl. When you board the train, ask the conductor the times of the return trains. In York, you'll find Hartwick's shop only a few yards from the railway station. Anyone can direct you. When you have the jewelry, wait in the shop until it is almost time to board the train. Once aboard, you will be quite safe. No one is going to rob you aboard a train, especially in broad daylight. And Lothar will meet the afternoon trains."

"Very well, your ladyship." Then Maryann's heart gave a leap. She just remembered something Lady Athaire had said at their first meeting. Marly-on-Willowbrook, the town where Jonathan Burke had spent his childhood, was on the railroad line leading to York.

22

A whistle blew, its sound rising above the hiss of steam from the engine. The train jolted forward. Seated with black-gloved hands folded in her lap, Maryann looked out the compartment window as the station platform, drenched with early sunlight, slid past.

The compartment door opened. Someone said, "Why, good morning!"

Maryann turned her head. Diane Olmstead stood in the doorway, chic in a blue-and-silver-striped dress and a blue bonnet trimmed with silver ostrich plumes.

"Good morning, Miss Olmstead."

"Are you going to York?"

"Yes."

Diane sat down. The train was half empty. Others might think it strange that she should choose to share the compartment of this American, this upper servant in her rusty black garments. But this particular servant—what was her name? Oh, yes, Mrs. Fallon—lived in the same house as Jonathan Burke.

"I'm going to York, too. Shopping." The dress she intended to wear for the Athaires' ball had been made in London. However, she had forgotten to order stockings to match it. Hence the trip to York. "You won't mind my sharing this compartment?"

"Of course not."

"I suppose you too intend to shop." High time she did, even if she were still in mourning. Mourning clothes could appear quite fashionable if properly cut. And according to Jonathan, the American was being paid a good salary.

"No, I'm not on a shopping trip." Even though she had guessed what the other young woman thought of her black dress, she remained unperturbed. She had more important things to do with her money than buy clothes. "I am on an errand for Lady Athaire."

Diane had enough good taste not to ask what sort of errand. "Will this be your first visit to York?"

Maryann nodded.

"It is a handsome city. In fact, Jonathan Burke told me that he likes it better than any other English city with the exception of London." She paused. "Do you see Mr. Burke very often? I suppose you must, living in the same house."

"I see him surprisingly little. I take my meals in my own sitting room, and the rest of time I am with Lady Athaire. Mr. Burke has his own affairs to attend to. I seldom see him except when we pass each other in the hallways."

For a moment she wondered what Diane Olmstead would feel if she knew where Maryann had last seen Jonathan Burke, standing behind that altar, face white with fervor

149

and blue eyes blazing as he gazed up at the inverted cross. Perhaps it would have little effect on Diane. Maryann sensed that the blond girl was obssessed with Jonathan, ready to forgive him anything and to do anything in order to obtain sole possession of him.

Diane waited, as if hoping that Maryann would say something more about Jonathan. When she did not, the English girl reached into her blue-and-silver-striped reticule and brought out a small paperbound volume. It was entitled *The Ordeal of Lady Esther*, Maryann saw, and its author was a Mrs. Humphrey-Price. After she opened the book, Diane said, "I've almost finished this. It's so exciting! Do you mind if I read for a while?"

"Not at all."

Diane read. Maryann watched the countryside slide past. Open fields dotted with sheep. Farmhouses, most of straw-thatched stone. Little villages, each with its tall church spire. Evidently this was a local train, because it stopped at every station.

The conductor appeared in the compartment doorway. He said, looking at Maryann, "Ma'am?"

"Yes?"

"You asked to be let off at Marly-on-Willowbrook. We will be there in about three minutes." He went down the corridor.

Maryann stood up. Diane said indignantly, "You told me you were going to York!"

"I am, by the next train. But I'm stopping over here until then."

Startled and alarmed out of even a pretense of good manners, Diane asked bluntly, "Why?"

"I have some business here."

Business? By what wild coincidence could this Mrs. Fallon have "business" to attend to in the small town where Jonathan Burke had lived as a child? Surely it was not a coincidence. Surely this "business" concerned Jonathan.

Maryann said, "Good-bye, Miss Olmstead. I hope you have a pleasant time in York." She walked away down the corridor.

Diane sat motionless. Had Elaine Athaire sent her secretary to this place on some sort of errand concerning Jonathan? Perhaps, but probably not. Probably the American was acting on her own. Like almost every female who saw him, she had fallen in love with him and was determined to find out more about him.

Diane had an impulse to follow the other girl. But already the train was in motion. Looking out, Diane saw Maryann talking to the ticket seller behind his grilled window.

Diane did not feel that Maryann was any threat as a rival. What could Jonathan possibly see in that thin, whey-faced creature? But in another way the American *was* a threat. She might unearth something about Jonathan's origins, something that would make it forever impossible for Diane to obtain parental consent to her marrying Jonathan. And this just at a time when her father seemed to be softening!

Only two nights earlier, perched on her father's knee, she had said, "You want me to be happy, don't you, Papa?"

He had beamed at her with the fondness that he had never displayed toward any of his sons. "That goes without saying, my pet." Suddenly he frowned. "You're thinking about Jonathan Burke, aren't you?" When she remained silent, he said, "You are being a foolish child, Diane. Why, in the first place, the fellow hasn't even proposed to you, has he?"

"But he would, Papa! If you gave him the slightest encouragement—"

"But in the meantime, he doesn't want to alienate Lady Athaire. Isn't that it?"

"Papa, all that gossip about him and Elaine is just that—gossip. He's pleasant to her and plays cards with her in the evening, but that is all. And it is wrong to look down on him because he's a steward. People say that the Athaire tenant farms never looked as well as they have since Jonathan and his assistant came to Windmere. He could be *your* steward, Papa."

She paused for breath and then went on. "As for his parents being shopkeepers—well, being a member of the gentry is no guarantee that a man has intelligence, or character, or anything else that is really important."

"You are right there, my love," he said dryly. "When I think of some of the young rakehells I know, men I'd never trust your happiness to—"

He paused, stared past her at the wall, and then said, "I'll have to think it over some more, my pet."

Now she tried to resume reading her book, but the printed words did not register on her mind. If Maryann Fallon or anyone else made additional difficulties just when she was about to get her father to change his mind—

She gripped the paper-covered novel so hard that a thread at the top of the binding gave way.

23

The greengrocer's shop to which the station ticket seller had directed Maryann smelled pleasantly of new potatoes in their tall baskets. Square containers filled with leeks and marrow and carrots and peas rested on the counter near one wall. Behind the counter stood a tall, dark-haired man of middle age.

Maryann asked uncertainly, "Mr. Burke?"

"Oh, no! I'm the clerk." He nodded at a doorless opening in the opposite wall. "Mr. and Mrs. Burke are upstairs."

She went through the doorway, climbed steep, uncarpeted stairs, knocked on a door. A man's voice called, "Come in."

She opened the door. A man seated at an oilcloth-covered table, an open ledger before him, looked at her for a startled moment and then got to his feet. He was gray-haired and thin and short, no taller than Maryann herself.

"Mr. Burke?"

"That is correct, ma'am. And over there is Mrs. Burke."

The gray-haired woman seated in a rocking chair, a basket of mending beside her, was also small. Maryann judged them to be in their late fifties. But seen from behind, she reflected, they would appear like half-grown children with prematurely gray hair.

Maryann said, "Forgive me for this intrustion. My name is Maryann Fallon—Mrs. Fallon—and I am secretary to Lady Athaire."

The pair exchanged an alarmed look. Then a certain blankness settled on their faces. Maryann had the feeling that they were prepared, from that point on, to lie to her.

Mr. Burke brought another rocking chair out from the wall. "Sit down, won't you?"

When Maryann was seated, Mrs. Burke laid the stocking she had been mending onto the pile of garments in the basket beside her. "Now, let me fix you a nice cup of tea."

"Oh, no, thank you. I haven't much time. I'm between trains on my way to York." She paused. "I've come about your son, Jonathan Burke. He looks so very much like my late husband that I can't help believing that they are related in some way."

They stared at her with that closed look on their faces. Then Mrs. Burke said, "They do say that everybody has a double, someplace in the world."

"But that's only a saying!" Then, less sharply: "You see, my husband too was born in this same general area. That is why it is so unlikely that your son's close resemblance to my late husband is mere happenstance."

Neither of the Burkes said anything. Maryann went on, rather desperately. "Forgive me for asking questions, but

154

the answers are vitally important to me. You see, I have a small son—"

She broke off and then said, "Your son resembles neither of you. That is why I wonder—and again, forgive me!—if he is your natural-born son."

There was no period of astounded silence, which such a statement should have caused. Instead, Mrs. Burke said quickly, "Of course he is ours. I should know, shouldn't I?"

"And he was baptized here in the village church?"

This time it was Mr. Burke who made the slightly-too-quick response. "He was."

"When he was how old?"

The answer did not come quickly. After perhaps half a minute Mr. Burke said, "He was nigh on six months, which is a little old for a baptism in this parish. But you see, he wasn't born in this village. He was born on a farm we had then. While Mrs. Burke was expecting, we decided to sell the farm and buy this shop. We didn't get the business completed until after Jonathan was born. What with the excitement of the baby, and moving into town, and stocking the shop, we didn't get around to the baptism right away. But we finally did. It's there in the record."

Maryann had no doubt that she would find such a record in the local church, with this pair listed as Jonathan's natural parents. But there was something wrong somewhere, something very wrong.

She looked at the clock on the mantelpiece and then got to her feet. "I must leave. The next train for York stops in a few minutes." She paused. "Would you like to send some sort of message to your son?"

155

Something flared in the small man's eyes for a moment, too briefly for Maryann to identify it. Then he said, "Just tell him we are both well and hope that he is."

"All right. Good-bye. Thank you both. And again, please forgive the intrusion."

She left. After a few moments Burke went to the window and looked down. The American woman was moving away along the sidewalk.

Behind him his wife spoke. "You think she's another one in love with Jonathan?"

"Not her!" He turned around. "She's a smart one, she is."

"Then why—"

"I believe what she told us. She thinks her husband was related to Jonathan. That would make her little boy related to him, too. And she's afraid of the idea. And hates it."

"She's a right to fear and hate," his wife said bitterly.

He sat down at the table and stared unseeingly at the outspread ledger. He was thinking of a chill April morning more than a quarter of a century in the past when, driving his empty cart along the road, he had spied what looked like a bundle of rags lying close to a meadow's low stone wall.

He had reined in. Even before he got out of the cart, he was sure what the bundle held. Although until now he had never happened upon one, he knew that infants occasionally were abandoned along this road. Lately, perhaps because times were hard, their number had increased. This child, wrapped in an ancient horse blanket, had been asleep. Somehow Burke had been sure right away that it was a boy. As Burke lifted the infant, it woke up, stared at the man's face from startlingly brilliant blue eyes, and then burst into howls.

Burke had intended to bring back a bushel or so of green peas from the field most distant from the farmhouse. But now he laid the infant carefully in the empty cart, climbed up onto the driver's seat, and headed back toward the house. Although married for eight years, he and his wife had had no child. And here by the roadside, like a gift from heaven, had been a man-child—a handsome one and, to judge by the volume of his howls, a healthy one.

By the time he reached the farmhouse, the child had stopped crying. Burke carried the baby in, exchanged a few excited words with his wife, and then laid the child on the kitchen table.

They both had feared that they would find some flaw—a large birthmark, say, or six-toed feet—that might have been the reason for his abandonment. But the child they unwrapped from the old blanket was perfect. Evidently pleased by the kitchen's warmth, he was kicking his legs and smiling.

Burke said, "How old do you think he is?"

Mrs. Burke, the eldest of ten children, answered promptly, "Three weeks, maybe four."

"He's a big 'un, for that age."

"He's going to be a big man, Jonathan is."

"Jonathan?"

She looked almost shyly at her husband. "I always thought if we ever had a son, I'd like to call him Jonathan."

He put his arm around her thin body and hugged her to him. "Then Jonathan he is."

"Get a blanket off the bed. Then we'll burn that filthy thing."

He brought the blanket. She transferred the naked infant to it, then swept the rough blanket in which he had been wrapped to the floor.

A metallic sound.

Burke bent, picked up something that shot red gleams. A ring, a ruby ring, its main stone surrounded with what looked like small diamonds.

Holding it on his palm, he said, "It looks like that ring we read about—"

"Yes. But put it on the mantelpiece. We have to attend to Jonathan."

They bathed the infant, diapered him with part of a sheet, fed him from a "sugar tit"—a small cylinder of cloth dipped in warm sugared milk and then held to the infant's lips until he began to suck. It was not until the child lay asleep in a blanket-lined basket that they turned their attention to the ring.

Burke said, turning it this way and that to catch the light, "It *must* be the one we read about."

"Yes. But how did it get inside that filthy blanket?"

"How should I know? Whoever left the child there must have wrapped the ring up with him." He paused. "Do you still have that copy of the *Yorkshire Chronicle?*" The *Chronicle* was a monthly publication devoted to sensationalism and the cause of electoral reform that was on sale in village tobacco shops and other establishments throughout the Yorkshire Ridings.

"No, I must have used that paper to kindle the fire months and months ago. The robbery was sometime last year, remember."

The memorable aspect of the event had been that it was

the sort of robbery that seemed to belong back in the eight-eenth century. In those days, when most people traveled by horse-drawn stage, highwaymen had been a scourge. The railroads had changed all that. But now and then people driving by private coach had been robbed. Lord Claypool had been one of them. Held at gunpoint by a masked man who had identified himself as Sidney Steve, both his lord-ship and his coachman had turned over what cash they had with them. In addition, Sidney Steve had demanded the one piece of jewelry his lordship was wearing, a large ruby ring bordered by diamonds.

Neither of the excited Burkes could remember what the *Chronicle* had said the ring was worth. Hundreds of pounds, anyway. Perhaps thousands.

The Burkes were not dishonest people. If they had found the ring lying in the road, they would have decided, how-ever reluctantly, to return it to his lordship, even though he was vastly wealthy and they were poor.

No, it was not the loss of the jewel they feared. It was the loss of Jonathan. If they gave up the ring and told the truth about where they had found it, the law in its majesty might decide to investigate the origins of the child, too, and return him to his natural parents, or parent.

"And that wouldn't be right," Mrs. Burke said passion-ately. "Whoever would leave a little baby at the roadside is wicked, wicked."

"Maybe his parents didn't do it. Maybe gypsies stole him and left him there."

"Gypsies? They might leave Jonathan by the roadside, but they wouldn't have wrapped that ring up with him. No!

We're not going to say anything about this to anyone. We'll keep Jonathan and the ring, too."

Excitedly and yet carefully, they made their plans.

Although Burke sometimes passed the time of day with other farmers he met on the road or on market day in the towns, Mrs. Burke saw almost no one. In fact, the last people to visit the isolated farm had been kinfolk of hers from Northumbria.

Burke said, "We can say that you've been expecting for more than four months now. You didn't want to tell even me because you were afraid we'd end up disappointed, the way we were that time five years ago. Anyway, that's the story I'll tell around. Then, a couple of months from now, I'll say the baby's been born, prematurelike."

"But if anyone sees him—"

"I think we can manage it that nobody will, not before we get away from here and move to Marly-on-Willow-brook."

They had discussed such a move several times during the past year, ever since Burke had injured his back in a fall from an apple tree in the farmyard. A greengrocer's shop was up for sale in Marly-on-Willowbrook. The asking price was high, but if they sold or mortgaged the farm, they could meet it. And tending shop would be much easier for a man with a bad back than farming.

Nevertheless, they had almost decided against the move. But now that shop, in a town twenty miles away, seemed irresistible. They knew no one there, and so no one would have any reason to doubt that Jonathan was their natural-born son.

"And the ring," Mrs. Burke said. "Probably we'll never

know why it was wrapped up with Jonathan in that old blanket. But it will be *his* ring. When he gets to the right age, we'll sell it and try to send him to one of those posh schools. He'll be a gentleman, our Jonathan will."

Everything went as they had planned. They moved to the town twenty miles away, took up residence above their greengrocer's shop, had Jonathan baptized. He gave such promise of strength and handsomeness that they not only loved him, they were a little in awe of him.

It wasn't until he was two that they began to feel a certain unease. Everyone said that two-year-olds were a handful. But was it normal for even a two-year-old, when restrained from some mischief, to sink his teeth into his mother's arm?

When he was five—surely old enough to know better— he cut off the tail of a newborn kitten with a meat cleaver. By the time he was seven, he was stealing coins from his parents to buy sweets. When he was nine and already about as tall as Burke, he launched upon his first sexual adventure. Down by the river one summer evening he encountered a ten-year-old girl who had wandered away from her family group. He caught her and tried to rip her blouse off. She escaped by leaving part of the ripped blouse in his hand. But when her outraged parents came to the Burkes' shop, bringing their daughter with them, Jonathan's angelically handsome face was so earnest and his blue eyes so tear-filled that even the girl, let alone her parents, began to be convinced that he was innocent and that it must have been someone else who tore her blouse.

(The Burkes were not convinced. By that time they had realized what sort of creature it was that Burke had picked up from the roadside that spring morning.)

161

When he was almost eleven and taller than Burke, he had knocked the aging man down and then stood over him with a brilliant smile and balled fists.

From then on, he ruled the small household. The Burkes' love for him, which had been close to adoration, had long since turned to loathing and fear. They lived for the day when Jonathan turned sixteen or thereabouts, decided that the village was too dull to hold him, and walked out of their lives.

They did not have to wait that long. Jonathan was still not eleven when the wealthy Mrs. Gaitsby, after nearly running him down in her carriage, fell completely under the spell of this tall young boy with the face of a Michelangelo David. Although he sometimes spent a few days with the Burkes during his vacations from that expensive boarding school, he stayed more often with his patroness or the family of one of his schoolmates. At Oxford he had followed the same pattern. His visits to the Burkes seldom lasted more than a few hours. But he did make such visits, even after he was a postgraduate, loafing around Oxford on the five hundred pounds Mrs. Gaitsby had left him, and even after he had become steward of Sir Rodney and Lady Athaire's estate. It was as if he enjoyed giving the two dull little people glimpses of his own brilliant life.

For some years now he had made it plain that he did not believe they were his real parents. "Even as a young boy," he had said during his visit of two months before, "I was sure you two hadn't produced me. Now, why don't you tell me who my real parents were?"

But the Burkes, looking him straight in the eye, insisted that he was their natural-born son.

162

At last he shrugged and got to his feet. "It makes no difference, really. As long as I can enjoy this world, why should I care how I got here?"

It was not any lingering pride in him, of course, that had made the Burkes determined that he would never know where and how they had found him. It was the ring, that ruby ring that, ever since Jonathan was an infant, had been hidden beneath a floorboard in the Burkes' bedroom. Even at this late date, they feared their possession of it might be discovered.

And in their bitterness over the way Jonathan had turned out, they were more determined than ever to hang on to the ring. In another year, both of them would turn sixty. They planned to sell the shop and cross the Channel to Holland. The favorite niece of Mrs. Burke lived there with her husband and three healthy, well-mannered children. After all these years and in a foreign country, it ought to be safe to sell the ring. The proceeds, plus the money from the sale of the shop, ought to keep them in modest comfort for the rest of their days. And whatever was left over would help her niece's children make a start in life.

Thus, that handsome monster would have brought some good into the Burkes' lives after all.

Now Burke said, "I hated to lie to that Mrs. Fallon. She seems like a nice young lady. But I felt we had to."

"Yes," his wife said, "we had to."

24

Driving the old farm cart, Maryann turned off the main highway onto the upward-sloping road. Seconds later, her nostrils were assailed by the first whiff of the pig farm smell.

It was through the special dispensation of Lady Athaire that Maryann was driving the cart. The afternoon before, still pleased by the banknotes as well as by the jewelry Maryann had brought back from York, she had smiled at her secretary's reflection in the dressing-table mirror. "What do you plan to do on Friday?" Friday was Maryann's day off.

"I shall walk to my mother-in-law's farm to visit her and my sister-in-law."

"Walk! But it is miles!"

"If I start out at daylight—"

"Nonsense." For a moment Maryann thought that her ladyship was going to offer the services of the coachman,

Lothar. Instead she went on, "You can drive a horse, can't you?"

"Certainly, your ladyship."

"Then have Lothar furnish you a cart and horse. I'm sure he can find something suitable."

On Friday morning Maryann waited beside Lothar outside the stable until one of the young grooms wheeled out an ancient cart. Lothar said, "Now bring out Samson."

As he spoke, she became aware that someone had joined them. She turned and saw Martin Cramer in riding clothes standing beside her. Her heart gave a little lurch.

He spoke not to her but to the groom. "No! Samson is still skittish, even if he is eight years old." His dark, unsmiling gaze moved to Maryann's face. "We wouldn't like to be responsible for your breaking your neck in a ditch."

Scarcely a graceful way of phrasing it. Still, it was all to the good that his manner remained cold. It helped her to ignore that stir of attraction he awoke in her.

Again he spoke to the groom. "Bring out Matty. She's safe enough."

As the groom walked away, Maryann said, "Thank you, Mr. Cramer."

He gave a brief nod, then followed the groom through the stable doorway.

Now, guiding the aged mare up the road between the pigpens, she reflected that Matty was indeed safe. Maryann could have made the journey almost as rapidly on foot.

Up the slope, Flora emerged from a pen, a bucket in each hand. Maryann reined in.

"So!" Flora gave that familiar, tight-lipped smile. "You've come to pay us a visit."

165

"How are you, Flora?"

"The same as always. Busy. Why don't you go up to the house and talk to Ma. I'll be with you later."

That suited Maryann exactly. It was really her mother-in-law she had come to see.

When she entered the low-ceilinged bedroom, the invalid's face lit up. She said, stretching out her arms, "Maryann! Come sit here, luv. No, not in the chair. On the edge of my bed."

They embraced. For a few minutes Maryann answered the woman's eager questions about Windmere, and what sort of work she did, and what her employer was like. Then, as soon as the questions had subsided, Maryann said, "Mother Fallon, I—I've been thinking about Jaimie's grandfather."

"Ian, you mean?" Expression flitted across the bed-ridden woman's face—a certain tenderness, then anger, then something that looked like amusement.

"Yes. What was he like?"

"A devil with the women. But I guess you knew that. Even when we were still living together, he was chasing girls. And when Flora was nine and Donald three, he just up and left."

"But you did hear from him, didn't you?"

"Oh, yes. Within a few months he sent me a letter from Liverpool with six shillings in it. Said he was working on the Liverpool docks for a company called World Wide Shipping. I couldn't read it, of course. Never did get the hang of reading and writing. But Flora could read by then."

"And he never came back?"

"Oh, yes! For a while he'd turn up for a few days every year or so. And between times, he often sent a few shillings.

Last time was seventeen years ago. His letter said he was still working on the docks, even though he was past sixty."

A shadow crossed her face, and Maryann knew that the invalid was wondering if her husband still lived. Then apparently some amusing memory struck her, because she chuckled and said, "Oh, but he was a devil!"

"What did he look like?"

Mrs. Fallon said promptly, "Like Donald. The last time I saw my boy, he was the spitting image of Ian when I first met him."

Which meant that Jonathan Burke was also the spitting image of Ian Fallon.

During one of his several returns to this area after his separation from his wife, Ian Fallon had almost certainly fathered another child, the boy who was to grow up as Jonathan Burke.

With her stomach tightening into a cold knot, Maryann asked, "Was there anything strange about your husband?"

"Strange? Well, I guess some would call his woman-chasing strange. Not many would have the strength for it."

"But aside from that?"

Mrs. Fallon frowned. "Well, he got drunk once in a while. Nothing else I can think of. 'Course, I didn't see much of him after those first ten years. Maybe he changed a lot after that." She paused and then asked half-humorously, "What's the matter? You afraid young James inherited bad blood?"

Before Maryann could frame a reply, her mother-in-law exclaimed, "Jaimie! How could I forget? A letter came for you from America last week. It must be about him. It's over there beside the washbasin."

167

Heart pounding with mingled joy and fear—after all, young children could fall prey to so many diseases—she seized the letter and tore it open. Her gaze flew down the page. Little James was in perfect health, Mrs. Yerxa had written. "And getting bigger every day. He'll be as tall as Donald, surely. I know this separation must be hard for you, but my daughter will bring him to you next summer. If you haven't saved enough for the fares by then, perhaps my husband and I can make you a loan. Just think, by the time you see your son, he'll be scampering all over the place. He's chattering like a magpie now."

The woman in the bed asked eagerly, "How is he?"

Maryann folded the letter and thrust it down the front of her dress. "He's doing very well indeed."

The letter had strengthened her resolve. As rapidly as possible, she was going to find out everything knowable about that strange creature—handsome, charming, and mentally twisted—who almost certainly was her child's half uncle.

She sat down on the bed's edge. "To get back to Jaimie's grandfather. Do you have any idea where he is now?"

"As I told you, last time he wrote he said he was still working on the docks. I guess he still is." Again a shadow crossed her face. "Unless he's dead, of course."

A step sounded in the outer room. "There's Flora," Mrs. Fallon said.

Maryann leaned over and kissed her mother-in-law's cheek. "I'd better help her in the kitchen."

A few yards away from the point where Maryann had turned off the highway toward the Fallon farm, a thin little man sat on a stone wall, partially hidden by the branches of a trailing beech. A dun-colored horse was tethered to a nearby sapling. Like his mount, the little man was nondescript, the sort no one ever looked at twice. That was why his services were in demand.

Keeping well back, he had followed the young widow until her cart turned off the highway toward the farmhouse. When she returned to the highway, he would again follow her. Just how long, he wondered, would he have to wait?

It was past five when Maryann returned to Windmere. She climbed from the ground floor to the landing of the rear staircase and then stopped short. A maid carrying a tray laden with a teapot and empty plates had just turned away from Lady Athaire's door.

At a quickened pace, Maryann walked down the hall. This would be a good time to make her request. Finished with tea and not yet launched upon her elaborate predinner toilette, her ladyship might be in an amiable mood.

She knocked on Elaine Athaire's door and then called softly, "Your ladyship? It's Maryann Fallon."

"Come in."

She found Lady Elaine stretched out on a chaise longue. Her chiffon tea gown was of light blue, the butterfly-shaped pin at her bosom a darker blue.

She asked, "How was your visit?"

"Pleasant." Aware that her employer could have no possible interest in the subject, she felt safe in making her reply brief. "Lady Athaire, I have a favor to ask of you."

The red-haired woman's eyebrows rose.

"I need to make a business trip to Liverpool. I'd like to go tomorrow, if possible."

Business trip. No doubt something to do with that revolting farm her sister-in-law kept. Lady Athaire thought of refusing, then decided to be gracious. After all, the girl had handled the matter of the emeralds very nicely. Besides, she would be making extra demands upon her secretary because of the upcoming ball. Her ladyship had a feeling that the American might be quite clever at arranging bouquets and floral garlands and so on, or at least cleverer than Mrs. Burnbeck, the housekeeper.

"Very well. But in return you may be asked to perform extra duties during the next few days."

"Gladly. Thank you, Lady Athaire."

In the cramped bedroom, Flora Fallon picked up an empty dish from her mother-in-law's washstand. It had held the old woman's supper, a portion of shepherd's pie.

Flora said, "So she took the letter with her."

"Yes. She said that little James is doing fine, just fine."

Flora already knew what the letter said. Days ago, she had steamed it open, read it, and resealed it.

Now, as she carried the empty dish into the main room, she thought of what the Yerxa woman had said about the little boy arriving in England next summer.

But suppose something happened. Suppose, for instance, that Jaimie's mother died. Then probably he would stay on his own side of the Atlantic. If so, the chances would be excellent that she, Flora, would eventually become the sole inheritor of the farm upon which she had worked so hard all her life.

25

Along the World Wide dock jutting out into Liverpool Harbor, ships flying the flags of a half-dozen nations were anchored. Most of them were sailing vessels. Tall masts, canvas furled tightly around them, swayed in such wide arcs against the late morning blue sky that it made Maryann dizzy to look at them. The long dock swarmed with men unloading bales of cotton, stalks of green bananas, crates that might have held almost anything. She saw one ship from Connecticut, the *Joseph Crail* out of New London. From its holds men were unloading bales of tobacco.

Men stared at her as she walked along, hoping to see someone who might be a contemporary of Ian Fallon's. But no one spoke to her or even made audible comments about her. That was one thing to be said for widow's weeds, she reflected wryly. A black dress and bonnet seemed to have a restraining effect even on dock workers.

A few yards ahead a man with a knitted red cap perched

on his white hair leaned against a stack of baled cotton. Oblivious to the danger to the inflammable cargo behind him, he was smoking a large clay pipe. Sparks blew from it in the stiff breeze. Maryann judged him to be an ex-longshoreman who still enjoyed the scene of his former labors.

She said, "Excuse me, sir."

The old man, startled, looked at her from faded blue eyes. Then he took the pipe stem from his mouth and gave her a gap-toothed smile. "Yes, ma'am!"

"I'm looking for a man named Ian Fallon. He works on the docks, or used to."

"Fallon! He used to work here, right enough, but I ain't seen him for two, three years. Guess the work got too much for him, even though he was younger than me." He raised his voice. "Joe! Joe Sims."

A burly man who appeared to be in his fifties lowered a crate from his arms to the rough planking. "Yes, Alfie?"

"You remember Ian Fallon?" The younger man nodded. "Lady here is looking for him."

Although his eyes were avidly curious, the burly man's voice was polite. "I ain't seen him for a long time, ma'am. I hear he's sick. But I can tell you where he and his missus live."

Maryann exclaimed involuntarily, "Missus!"

The burly man's expression was half embarrassed, half amused. "Well, that's what she calls herself. Anyway, they live close to here. Turn right after you get off the docks and walk maybe a hundred and fifty yards. You'll see a ship chandler's shop. Ian lives on the floor above."

She thanked both men. Aware of covert masculine glances, she walked rapidly toward the street.

A few minutes later she was climbing narrow but quite clean steps and knocked on a door. It opened promptly. A plump woman with graying brown hair stood silhouetted in the light from the window behind her. Maryann judged her to be in her midfifties.

"Yes?"

"Does Ian Fallon live here?"

The woman's eyes narrowed. "Who's asking for him?" She paused. "I'm his missus."

Maryann didn't dispute that. Fleetingly, she reflected that the invalid on that isolated farm probably would not mind too much that this woman was making such a claim. Probably she would just chuckle and say that it was some more of Ian's devilment.

"My name is Fallon, too. My husband was Donald Fallon, Mr. Ian Fallon's son."

Still the woman did not invite her in. Her gaze moved from her visitor's face down to her shoes and then back again. Maryann thought, Why, she's jealous! Jealous of a sick man at least twenty years her senior.

Perhaps his wife was right. Perhaps Ian really did have a way with women.

Reluctantly the woman opened the door wider. "Come in."

Maryann stepped into a clean, sparsely furnished room that evidently served as parlor, dining room, and kitchen. "Ian's in the bedroom. You may have trouble talking to him. You see, he's not right in the head."

Maryann's stomach tightened into a cold knot. "You mean he has become insane?"

"Oh, no. He just can't remember things sometimes. Or people. You see, about a year ago he had a shock. It makes it hard to understand him when he talks, too."

For a moment Maryann felt puzzled. Then she recalled

that in Connecticut, too, some people called a paralytic stroke a shock.

The woman said, "You're not going to upset him, are you?"

"I hope not. I'll certainly try not to. It's just that I want to ask him some questions. You see, it's for the sake of my little boy."

The woman's face softened. "You've got a little boy? Ian's grandson? I hope you can make him understand that. He'd like it." Her voice became stern. "But don't you upset him."

"As I told you, I'll try not to."

The woman opened a door, beckoned. Maryann looked in. Her heart lurched. A man sat in an armchair, gray head tilted back, eyes closed. Although heavily lined, his face was handsome, the classic features strong, the jaw square. This was the way Donald would have looked someday, if fate had allowed them to grow old together.

"Ian," the woman said softly.

The man's eyes opened. Blue eyes, startlingly young in contrast to the deep facial lines and to something Maryann noticed for the first time—a slight droop at the left side of his mouth.

"Here's someone to see you, Ian." She turned to her visitor. "Sit in that chair beside him."

The woman moved back into the front room. Pointedly, though, she left the connecting door open.

Maryann walked to the straight chair near her father-in-law, sat down. Still looking at her with those blue, blue eyes, he gave her a one-sided smile.

"I'm Maryann Fallon, your son Donald's wife."

His gaze was friendly but not fully comprehending. He said, slurring the words, "Donald went to America."

174

"Yes, and married me."

Evidently the significance of her black garments had not registered on his injured brain. Well, she decided swiftly, there was no need to tell him of his son's death.

"Donald and I had a little boy. Your grandson's name is James."

The self-styled Mrs. Fallon had said that if he understood about the grandson, he would be glad. Evidently he had not understood. His expression remained the same, pleasantly serene. Well, she had tried.

She said, "You have another son. His name is Jonathan."

She spoke swiftly, afraid that the woman listening in the next room might intervene. She did not. Apparently his living companion was already aware that Ian might have other than legitimate offspring.

He said, "Jonathan?"

"Jonathan Burke. Burke was the name of the people who raised him."

Ian's face lit up. "Jonathan Burke!" he said in that slurred voice. "I heard about him once when I was home." He must have been referring to one of his rare visits to the Fallon farm and its vicinity. "Burke. Greengrocer's shop. Went there to see if I could get a look at him. He was playing out front. Lad of about five. Spitting image of me."

"Who told you he was there? His mother?"

"Mother?" His voice, animated only a moment ago, was pleasantly vague.

"Jonathan's mother. Did she tell you where Jonathan was?"

"Could be. I don't recollect."

She leaned forward. "Who was Jonathan's mother? What was her name?"

For the first time he frowned—not with displeasure, she sensed, but in an effort to gather his stroke-addled wits. "I don't recollect." Then his face lit up. "But she was a great one for butterflies." His chuckle seemed to hold a ribald note. "A great one."

Maryann sat stunned.

Elaine Athaire.

Oh, she could understand how it happened. Ian Fallon, a man of superlative handsomeness, and still in his prime. Elaine Athaire, married to a plump, rather foolish man whose only attraction was his title. And despite the title her marriage had brought to her, the social disparity between herself and Ian was negligible. He had been raised on a sheep farm, she in rooms above a dyer's shop.

The two could have met for the first time almost anywhere—while she was out horseback riding, or while she was at one of those county fairs where, by tradition, the gentry put in an appearance. After that, secret trysts.

There were two things, Maryann reflected, that she probably would never know—how Elaine Athaire had concealed from the world the result of their adulterous union, and how the child had come into the hands of the Burkes. At least, she would never find it out from the vaguely smiling man she sat beside now.

As for Jonathan Burke's relations with her employer, Maryann had assumed they were lovers. Now she felt that that could not possibly be. She found the idea of even unwitting incest unthinkable, and in this case it could not be unwitting. Elaine could not help but know that Jonathan was Ian Fallon's son. He bore the stamp of his paternity in every feature.

So that was why she had induced her husband to hire him and to keep him on as steward, even though it was Martin Cramer who did the actual work. That was why she continued those after-dinner card games she almost always lost. She had been indulging a son, not a young lover.

But it was another thought that kept Maryann sitting there in appalled and wretched silence. She had come to know her employer quite well. Elaine Athaire was vain, extravagant, and, except for a certain low cunning where getting her own way was concerned, rather stupid. But madness, the sort of madness Maryann had seen in Jonathan's face, as he stood at the ruined abbey's altar? There was no trace of that in Elaine Athaire.

So it was through Ian Fallon that the seed of madness had been passed down. Never mind that his wife, Donald's mother, had said that aside from being "a devil with the women" there had been nothing "wrong" with Ian. And never mind that the woman in the next room had said that it was not until his "shock" that Ian had become "not right in the head."

Would that seed of madness later have flowered in his elder son? Because she had loved Donald so deeply, it was hard for her to believe that he could ever have resembled his half-brother in anything but appearance. Now, though, she forced herself to face the possibility.

And Jaimie? What of her little son?

She had to get out of here, away from that man in the armchair. She stood up.

Except for the slurring, Ian's voice sounded like that of anyone bidding a visitor a polite farewell. "Nice of you to come to see me, Sally."

She wondered which of all the women he had known had been named Sally, and why, at the last moment, he had thought she was that woman.

She nodded and went into the other room.

Ian's companion stood beside a rocking chair, one hand gripping its back. Beside her the hands of a white china clock on a small table pointed to a quarter of eleven.

The woman said, "You found out what you wanted to know?"

Unable to speak, Maryann nodded.

"Who is this Jonathan you asked him about? Somebody you're setting your cap for?"

"No!" Then, swiftly: "I must get to the omnibus stop. My train leaves at noon. Good-bye, Mrs. Fallon. Thank you."

Fifteen minutes later, as the plodding horses drew the omnibus over Liverpool's cobblestones, Maryann had a sudden sensation that someone's gaze was fixed on the back of her head. The feeling was so strong that she turned and looked.

No one was paying any attention to her. In the seat behind her, a woman fussed with the bonnet of the child on her lap. Across the aisle and back a few seats, two women were in low-voiced conversation. Behind them, a thin, nondescript man was reading from a small volume that could have been anything from a prayer book to a railway guide.

Turning to look straight ahead, she concentrated on her own wretched thoughts.

26

Sunset light was gilding the garden roses when Maryann, tired after her dusty two-mile walk from the village, came through the gate in the hedge. She was hungry, too, despite her unhappiness. That morning she had told Jenny, the middle-aged maid who brought her meals, that she would be away possibly until eight that night. "Then there's no use in my leaving hot food for you," Jenny said. "I'll tell Cook to fix something cold for you." But even a cold meal would be welcome.

She went in the rear entrance, climbed to the servants' floor. Her dinner tray sat on the table near the window. Cold sliced mutton, sliced tomatoes, a small bun. Hardly a banquet, but it would taste good tonight.

At her dressing table in the bedroom she removed her bonnet. Then it dropped to the floor. Reflected in the mirror, a man stood in the far corner of the room, smiling at her.

She whirled around. He walked toward her. In the shadows now filling the room, his hair looked bright.

She said, "What are you doing in my room?"

"I knew you would say exactly that. It's one of the most predictable of female utterances. And the most hypocritical. You know exactly why I'm here." He paused. "Even a sixteen-year-old would know, and you are scarcely that, are you?"

Her voice shook. "Get out."

He stood inches from her now. "And if I don't, you will—what? Scream? Then you would be in trouble, not me. No one is going to dismiss me for this. Not that poor sod, Sir Rodney. And certainly not Lady Athaire. *You* are the one she would get rid of. And then it would be back to the pig farm for you, my girl."

She said in a thickened voice, "Don't touch me."

He saw fear and loathing in her eyes. The fear he rather liked. He had often seen in women's eyes a fascination touched with fear. But the loathing infuriated him. How was it that she, this penniless widow in her cheap mourning clothes, could despise him? Why, she should be flattered that he even looked at her.

Angrily he caught her to him, his right arm imprisoning both of hers. His left hand forced her face around, thumb and fingers pressing into her cheeks. His kiss was prolonged, bruising her lips against her teeth.

A shudder ran through her whole body. The most terrible part was not that she knew it was a kind of monster who held her. Even more horrifying was the fact that the monster wore Donald's face.

She got one arm free, swung wildly, struck the side of

180

his face with her open palm. Startled, he relaxed his grasp slightly.

She wrenched free of him, heard a ripping sound as her dress gave way at the shoulder. Whirling about, she dodged around a footstool, heading for the doorway. In the darkened room he did not see the footstool. As she ran across her sitting room, she heard the sound of his fall.

She jerked her door open. Out in the corridor, she ran toward the back stairs. She was near the bottom of the flight when she heard his pursuing footsteps. Not knowing where she should go, only knowing that she could not bear to have him touch her again, she ran down the taper-lighted corridor, past the door to Sir Rodney's room, past Martin Cramer's door, and Jonathan Burke's—

Someone appeared at the head of the stairs leading up from the ground floor. He halted, then strode toward her. She slackened her pace.

Martin Cramer's voice was sharp. "What is the trouble, Mrs. Fallon?" Then, looking past her, "What is all this?"

Jonathan said, in a tone that didn't even ask to be believed, "I paid a call on the lady. She misunderstood my intent. I was trying to catch up to her to explain."

Martin's dark gaze rested on the ripped shoulder of Maryann's dress. "I don't think the lady misunderstood." His voice turned very cold. "And here is something you had best not misunderstand. If you annoy her again, you will be sorry indeed."

Jonathan smiled, although his eyes were raging. "Aren't you rather absurd, old man? I outweigh you and outreach you, and besides—" He broke off and then added, "Or does a hero ignore a little thing like a bad leg?"

His smile very wide now, he began to quote the Tennyson poem about the day that had left Martin Cramer with a limp.

" 'Half a league, half a league / Half a league onward / All in the valley of death / Rode the six hundred—' "

Martin said, "Never mind the six hundred. It's the Rossiter two thousand you had best worry about."

Jonathan's smile vanished. Alarm as well as anger in his eyes now. Then after a moment he again smiled. "Sorry, old man. If I had known you were *that* interested in the lady yourself, I would never have intruded."

Turning, he walked to his door, opened it, and went inside, closing the door quietly.

Martin said, "May I take you to your rooms?"

Still unable to speak, Maryann nodded.

They walked back along the hall, climbed the stairs. When they reached her door, he said, "May I come in? I have something to say to you."

"Very well. But first of all, thank you for what you did."

He nodded, opened the door. When she had walked past him into the room, almost completely dark now, he said, "Where are your matches?"

"Right there, on the stand beside the door."

The gas jet flared. Suddenly she was aware of her torn sleeve. She clasped her hand over her bare shoulder. "My dress!"

"If it will make you feel better, I'll pin it for you."

Both of them standing beside her dressing table, he took pins from the little glass tray she pointed out to him. She found something appealing in the way he accomplished the small task, his fingers careful not to touch her bare shoulder.

When the pins were in place, he accompanied her back into the sitting room. She gestured toward the two chairs flanking the small table beside the window.

He said, "Here's your dinner!"

Sinking into a chair, she said, "I don't want it now."

He didn't argue, just took the tray and placed it out in the hall. He closed the door and then sat down opposite her.

"Mrs. Fallon, I owe you an apology. I've had some erroneous and very unjust notions about you."

Her voice trembled a little, but she managed to smile. "I know. You thought that Sir Rodney— You thought that I—"

"Yes. I also felt that you took an immediate interest in Jonathan Burke."

"I did! But not *that* kind of interest. It was terrible, that first time I saw him. For a few seconds I thought he was —he was my Donald, come back to life. And then I looked into his eyes, and I saw that he wasn't even anyone like Donald. He was evil, evil!"

The day's events overwhelmed her. Bursting into tears, she put her hands up to her face.

He made no move toward her. Instead he said quietly, "Cry as much as you need to, Mrs. Fallon. Then we will talk."

A few minutes later she drew out a handkerchief, dried her tears, restored the handkerchief to the pocket of her dress.

He asked, "Do you want to tell me about it?"

She found that she did, very much. In a voice still a little hoarse from her weeping, she began to talk. Donald's death.

Her sister-in-law's farm. The mine with its grotesquely dwarfed young girl workers. And again, her shock at first sight of Jonathan Burke.

When she told Martin about her surreptitious visit to the ruined abbey that night, she could tell from his expression that he already knew about those secret ceremonies. In fact, she realized, that was why he had wanted her to stay away from the place.

She spoke of her conviction that Jonathan was mad and her growing need to find out what his origins were. She told of her visit to the Burkes in their greengrocer's shop and then of her talk with her mother-in-law a few days later.

"And then today I went to Liverpool to try to find Ian Fallon." Her voice not only hoarse but exhausted now, she told of her conversation, such as it had been, with the stroke-addled man.

At last Martin said sharply, "Are you sure he said 'a great one for butterflies'?"

"I'm sure."

From the stunned look on Martin's face, she knew that he, too, had never dreamed that Jonathan could be Elaine Athaire's son.

"So you see," Maryann said, her tired voice dull now, "it must be that Jonathan Burke inherited his madness from his father. Certainly he could not have from his mother. Lady Athaire may not be very intelligent, but what brains she has are sound enough. And that means that my little boy—"

"But it doesn't, not necessarily. After all, you said that your husband, Jonathan's half-brother, was not only a fine

184

man but a thoroughly sound one. I don't know much about such matters, but I do recall reading that even when an inheritance of insanity can be traced, it can skip individuals or even entire generations."

She nodded, a little comforted even though not convinced. She said, "To get back to Jonathan. You said something that frightened him. Something about the Russells and two thousand—"

"Rossiter. Young Lord Rossiter. At Oxford, Jonathan stole two thousand pounds from Rossiter's rooms. His idea was to bet the money on a certain steeplechase and win enough to put the money back and still have a fortune. The horse lost."

"How did you know—"

"Jonathan told me one night when he was drunk. Young Rossiter is a grandson of one of the Royal Dukes and therefore a cousin of the Queen's. If Jonathan's theft became known, no one could protect him, certainly not people like the Athaires."

"You never told anyone until now?"

Martin shrugged. "Young Rossiter is no good. Oh, not as depraved as Jonathan, but still no good."

Maryann wondered if Rossiter had been one of those cowled men at the abbey that night.

Martin went on. "I saw no reason to get mixed up in it. But now—"

He broke off and then said, "I'm going to be away for a few days. Cumberland. Some cattle are coming up for auction there. I hope to buy about a hundred head."

"A hundred head of cattle! Where will you—"

"They will be part of a shipment of cattle—several shiploads, in fact—going to a Texas port on the Gulf of Mexico. I've made tentative plans for a rancher there to take charge of them until I arrive."

"You're going to America?"

"I hope to." He smiled wryly. "All I am sure of is that I will be in Cumberland for a few days." He got to his feet. "I had best say good night now."

She accompanied him to the doorway. He said, turning, "I'm sure Jonathan won't dare bother you. But still—"

"Still what?"

He smiled briefly. "I don't know. It's just a feeling. But take good care of yourself until I get back. Will you promise?"

"Yes."

They stood looking at each other. He did not draw her to him, did not kiss her, and yet she felt that he had, and that she had liked it.

For the first time, he called her by her Christian name. "Good night, Maryann."

"Good night, Martin."

She looked after him as he walked away with that slight limp. Then she closed her door and leaned against it. She said aloud, "Forgive me, Donald. Perhaps it is just that I am so lonely."

It seemed to her that in her heart she heard his voice: "I know, my darling, I know. And there is nothing to forgive."

27

During the next week Maryann worked hard enough to more than make up for that extra day off. As the night of the ball approached, Lady Athaire became increasingly agitated. Again and again she told Maryann to drop whatever she was doing and take instructions to the housekeeper. Often they were the exact opposite of instructions she had issued an hour or so before. She also ordered her secretary to ask the gardener which roses would be at their best the night of the ball and then devise plans for a dozen bouquets, each different from all the others, for the salon. Maryann even joined her ladyship's personal maid on a search for a silver buckle, unaccountably missing from the pair of green satin slippers their employer planned to wear for the great occasion. They finally found it in a corner where, behind a drapery, Pompom was in the habit of leaving small objects after he grew bored with batting them about over the carpet.

Maryann did not mind the extra work or the semihysterical atmosphere. In fact, she welcomed it. It was a distraction from her own unhappy thoughts.

One thing she was most grateful for. That whole week she did not see Jonathan Burke, except at a distance. He did not come to her employer's rooms during the hours when she herself was there, nor did he—at least, not as far as she knew—climb to the servants' floor.

Several times that week Maryann managed to slip away from the house for brief periods. While her ladyship took a pre-teatime nap, Maryann would walk down to the quarry. Even if the day was overcast, she would sit on the flat rock for a few minutes to watch the swallows circle and dive.

Although she always found the place deserted, twice she had the same feeling that had come to her on the omnibus in Liverpool, a sense of someone watching her. Each time her gaze swept the low surrounding hills. Was Luddy up there someplace, her small figure crouched behind a gorse bush? Ever since the day Maryann had encountered her along the path to the quarry, daisies stuck in her tangled hair, she had seen no sign of Luddy. Still, she might have decided to amuse herself with a bit of spying upon the American newcomer.

For Maryann, the day of the ball was a disaster from its outset. The maid who brought Maryann's breakfast—a new maid, broad-faced and clumsy-looking—said, "There's somebody to see you. She'd down in the stableyard. She says she's your sister-in-law."

Her heart hammering with the fear that Flora had received some bad news about Jaimie, Maryann hurried out to the stableyard. Flora sat in the old cart that was used on the Fallon farm. The farm's one horse, a swaybacked grey mare named Dora, stood between the traces.

Flora said, almost without preamble, "I've come to see if you can loan me a few shillings."

"Flora! You know I'm trying to save every penny so that—"

"Two of the pigs I was fattening for market died. I was counting on that money to see us through the next few months." She paused. "You wouldn't want Donald's mother to go hungry, would you?"

Maryann shook her head.

"Even five shillings would help."

Maryann went upstairs, came back with the money, and handed it to Flora. "Ta," Flora said, putting the money in her skirt pocket. "Well, I'd better get back to the Brooders."

"The Brooders?"

"Farmers near here. Athaire tenant farmers, matter of fact. I've known them for years. I'll spend the day with them and maybe even tonight. A round trip in one day is too much for old Dora here."

"But Mother Fallon—"

"I asked one of the Thompson girls to stay with her until I got back. You remember the Thompsons."

Maryann nodded. The Thompsons, a couple with three daughters, all of them under twelve, lived about a mile from the Fallon farmhouse. She said good-bye to Flora and then, trying not to think of the lost shillings, hurried into the house. She could only hope that Lady Athaire was not awake and demanding her services.

She was in luck there. When she reached Elaine Athaire's

rooms, her ladyship had just awakened and needed only the services of her personal maid. But after that Maryann's luck changed. Around eleven o'clock, Pompom got out.

It was Maryann's fault. At least, Lady Athaire felt it was. Maryann was just about to leave her ladyship's sitting room with still another message for the housekeeper when her ladyship said, "Wait!"

Her hand on the knob of the half-open door, Maryann turned toward her employer. Pompom shot through the opening.

"You stupid creature!" Elaine Athaire cried. Then: "Catch him, catch him! Don't let him get to the stables."

Maryann darted into the hall. A plumy tail was disappearing down the back stairs. She reached the landing just in time to see him streak past the gardener's young assistant, who, laden with a potted palm, had come through the rear entrance.

She plunged down the staircase and out onto the terrace. Pompom, thank heaven, hadn't headed for the stables. Instead, he was turning the corner of the house.

Desperately she chased after him. A housemaid appeared around the front corner of the house. Seeing his avenue of escape cut off, the cat whirled, took a flying leap, and landed on the giant old wisteria vine that clung to Windmere's gray stone wall. Halting, Maryann watched with dismay as the animal scrambled upward for about twenty feet and then, with another leap, disappeared inside an open window.

The housemaid, a scrawny girl of about seventeen, had also halted. "Wot yer goin' to do?" Dismay in her voice. Evidently she, too, realized that the very success of the ball might depend upon returning the cat to his distraught mistress. How could Lady Athaire give her full mind to entertaining her guests when Pompom might have been savaged by the stableyard toms?

Maryann looked up at the window. Its draperies were drawn.

That was odd. On a hot, sunny morning, draperies might be drawn on this, the eastern side of the house, to keep the rooms cool. But there was no sunlight this morning. In fact, an overcast sky threatened rain, a circumstance that of course added to Lady Athaire's agitation. It was impossible for Maryann to tell to which room the window belonged. Perhaps one of the guest rooms on that floor. Should she hurry into the house, climb to that floor, and begin opening doors? No, even if she did find the right room, Pompom would hear her opening the door and escape again.

She gazed at the wisteria vine. It looked as if it had been there for at least a hundred years. Probably it had. Its meandering branches, thick as a man's forearm, appeared stout enough to support her weight.

"I'm going after him," she said.

She began to climb, hampered only a little by her long skirts. When her feet were on a level with the windowsill, she transferred the grasp of her right hand, then her left, from the vine to the thick draperies. Praying the drapery rod would hold, she stepped onto the sill and then, still clinging to the thick material, let herself down into the room.

By the light of the gas jet, Sir Rodney had been standing before the open doors of the wig cupboard, making his selection. Absorbed by the task, he had been unaware of

Pompom's silent entrance. But now he whirled around, consternation in his face.

Struck dumb, Maryann stared at the man whose hoop-skirted gown of red satin was topped by a bald head, glistening in the gaslight.

He looked ridiculous, of course, and yet she felt no impulse toward laughter.

A memory stirred, a dim one from her eighth year. Her father's housekeeper and another woman had been talking in the kitchen. Sitting unnoticed on the back step with her doll, Maryann had heard the visitor say, "Did you hear about Paul Winship?"

"The oldest Winship boy, the one who went to New York?"

"That's him. They say he's in Paris now, making a lot of money on the stage. He wears dresses and gives imitations of famous actresses."

"No! Well, I heard he used to dress up like that in the Winship attic, but he didn't make any money at it." Both women laughed.

Later Maryann had repeated the conversation to her father. After a long moment he said, "Don't worry about it, my darling. Yes, I've heard that some men like to wear women's clothing. I suppose some would say it is a sort of sickness of the mind. I don't know. I am not an alienist. But I do feel it is not a sin in the way cruelty and avarice and thievery are sins. And don't repeat such conversations, Maryann. It is what is called gossip, and gossip is almost always unkind."

Now Sir Rodney was looking at her through the gaslight with terror and hatred. He had been having such a wonderful time picturing himself at the ball tonight, not in the somber black and white of male evening attire but in this latest creation of a leading Paris couturier. And now this! She could ruin him, he thought frantically, utterly ruin him! How he wished he had left her back there in those pigpens, with her skirts hiked up and mud on her bare legs.

His voice was thick. "What are you doing here?"

"Pompom," she said, her gaze darting wildly about the room. "He got out, and Lady Athaire told me to get him back—"

She saw the cat now. He sat on a table in one corner, calmly grooming an outstretched rear leg.

"Take him," Sir Rodney said in that same thick voice. "Take him and get out of here." Turning, he twisted the heavy key in the door lock.

She walked to the cat and gathered him into her arms. His appetite for adventure temporarily satisfied, he did not resist.

As she walked toward the door, Sir Rodney said, "If you tell anyone about this, I'll make you sorry you were ever born."

She looked into the aging, desperate face. She said, meaning it, "I won't tell anyone."

He repeated, not believing her, "Sorry you were ever born."

He opened the door slightly, poked his head out, looked in both directions. He withdrew his head and said, "Leave! Quickly!"

Carrying her furry burden, she slipped out into the empty hall and turned toward Lady Athaire's rooms.

28

The five-piece orchestra arrived by coach a little after eight. The musicians set up their instruments in the flower- and palm-bedecked salon, now cleared of all its furniture except for rows of fragile-looking gilt chairs lined up along the walls. The guests began to arrive at nine. Maryann, who had slipped down to the floor below her own, watched from the stair landing as Sir Rodney and his wife greeted the first arrivals. Lady Athaire looked so calm in her green satin gown and her emeralds that no one would have dreamed she had been half-hysterical with various anxieties, ranging from Pompom's flight to the breaking of a corset string less than an hour earlier. Sir Rodney's face above his gleaming white shirtfront also looked composed, but even from that distance Maryann could sense his unhappiness and fear.

She walked to the back stairs and went up to her room. She had thought that a belated cold supper might have been brought to her. Apparently, in all the excitement, no one had thought to bring her anything. She went down three flights and slipped into the kitchen, crowded tonight with extra staff. She filled a plate with cold sliced ham and some cheese and bread and carried the food back to her room.

By that time the rain that had threatened all day was falling, gently at first, then with increasing violence. Well, at least it had held off until after the ball started. She drew the double-paned windows shut and fastened them. Perhaps it was the strain of the day, but she was so tired, she barely had the energy to finish her meal. She changed into a nightdress, extinguished the gas jet, and got into bed. Despite the drum of rain mingling with faint strains of music from two floors below, she fell asleep almost immediately.

An unmeasured interval later, her dreaming self wandered over moorland. A white mist rose from the ground, an evil mist that stung her nostrils and choked her lungs. What had happened, why was she out here, and what was it, this choking, burning mist? And how could she escape it? It hovered a few feet above the ground in every direction.

She stumbled forward over the rough earth. Then she began to moan, and her moaning woke her up.

Her own bed. Darkness. The hard pounding of rain against the windowpanes. Her own room, not a mist-shrouded moor. And yet she could still smell the mist, and it was still hard for her to breathe—

Gas.

Dizzily she sat up in bed, swung her feet to the carpet. When she stood up, she was so unsteady that she nearly pitched forward onto her face. Automatically her hand groped for the robe she had placed over a chairback. Trailing the garment over the rug, she stumbled across the sitting room to the door.

The door lock, like many of the appointments in these rooms assigned to her, had been long neglected. Sometimes it would close firmly and easily and open the same way. Other times it resisted her. Now, increasingly frantic in the gas-thickened air, she tugged at the knob, tugged again. Could someone have locked it from the outside? Suddenly it gave way, and she almost fell out into the hall.

Not really knowing what she did, only wanting to get away from that deadly gas, she broke into a stumbling run. Where were the stairs? After a moment she realized she had turned the wrong way, toward the front staircase. Never mind. The important thing was to get to the floor below.

She started down the stairs, tripped over the robe she carried in her hand, fell headlong. She let out a cry. Her plunge to the landing below did not really hurt her, although the blow that her forehead struck against the hall baseboard left her momentarily stunned.

Then she heard a babble of voices. There must have been an interval in the music, because her outcry had been heard, and now people were coming up the stairs from the main floor. She managed to get to her feet and was struggling into her robe when the first person reached the landing. He was Sir Rodney, with his wife close behind him.

Now others had crowded onto the landing. Most of them were strangers to her, but she was dazedly aware that Diane Olmstead was there, exquisite in ice-blue satin, and Jonathan Burke, his blond head rising inches above any of the others. Agnes, the new maid who had brought her breakfast that morning, hovered at the crowd's edge.

Lady Athaire exclaimed, "Maryann! What is the meaning of this?"

"Gas," Maryann said from a throat that felt raw. She had managed to pull her old blue flannel robe close around her, aware as she did so of how strange she must look among these gorgeously arrayed people. "Gas escaping in my rooms."

"Escaping! From the jet? You must have made a mistake. You blew it out instead of turning it off." Then, to Sir Rodney: "Take our guests back downstairs, dear. Enjoy yourselves, everyone. I will be with you as soon as I straighten this out. No, don't you go, Jonathan. I need you. Will you go up to Maryann's rooms? Turn off the jet if it is still on and open the windows if they are closed.

"Agnes, take Mrs. Fallon up to the room opposite hers. It is empty, I think. Stay there with her until her own quarters are free of gas."

Despite her dazed state, Maryann realized that her employer no longer sounded annoyed. Perhaps she had decided that the incident added a spice of excitement to the ball. Or perhaps she felt proud that, before witnesses, she had handled the situation well.

Jonathan's long stride had already carried him to the floor above. Lady Athaire said to Maryann, "Be more careful after this. I realize you probably aren't very used to gas illumination. But try to remember. Turn the gas off. Never blow out the flame."

Maryann thought it best to say as little as possible. "Yes, Lady Athaire."

"Good night." Elaine Athaire descended the stairs toward her guests. Agnes put a supporting arm around Maryann's waist while they climbed to the servants' floor. As

197

they neared Maryann's rooms, Jonathan Burke emerged and walked toward them.

"I turned off the jet and opened the windows. The rooms should be clear of gas soon." His smile was brilliant, but his eyes were cold, hating.

"Thank you," Maryann said, not smiling at all.

She and Agnes went into the room opposite Maryann's. The maid took matches from a table just inside the door and lighted a gas jet. This room, Maryann saw, was smaller and more shabby than either of her own rooms. They sat down on a small sofa with faded upholstery and sagging springs. Many years ago, probably, the sofa had seen service on the ground floor.

Agnes said, "Do you think her ladyship could have been right?" She hesitated, as if not knowing whether to call her ma'am or not. She finally compromised by adding, "Mrs. Fallon."

"About what?"

"You blowing the light out."

"I really don't know."

She had been thinking about it. It was true that most of the time while she was growing up the parsonage had been lit by oil lamps and candles. She had been sixteen before the board of elders decided to install gas. And when she and Donald had set up housekeeping at the farm, they of course had had only oil lamps. At the Fallon farm, light had been furnished by homemade tallow candles, and sparingly at that. When you worked from dawn to dark, you needed light only to eat and undress by.

Had she, because of that stressful day, become exhausted

to the point that she had regressed to earlier habits and extinguished the light by blowing it out?

Now she said, "I think I will see if my rooms—"

She crossed the hall to the wide-open door of her sitting room. There was not even the faintest lingering smell of gas. She lit the jet beside the door. Rain, more moderate now, was blowing in the open windows. Well, let it. She would dry the carpets as best she could in the morning.

She walked back across the hall. "It's all right now, Agnes. Good night, and thank you very much."

A few minutes later, in her own bed, she lay wide awake. Suppose she had not blown out the gas. Suppose she had extinguished it in the proper way, by turning off the jet.

In that case, someone must have turned it on again.

She pictured someone opening the door to her sitting room, softly, carefully. Perhaps tiptoeing as far as her bedroom door to be sure that there, too, the windows were closed against the rain. Then retreating to the gas jet, turning it on, and, after slipping out into the hall, gently closing the door.

But who?

She realized that it could have been any one of scores of people. The house had been full, not only of ball guests but also of extra people the Athaires had hired—the musicians and additional waiters and footmen. Any of them could have slipped up to this floor for the necessary few moments.

What was more, if the rear entrance tonight had been guarded by that irresponsible young footman, almost anyone could have gotten in. Right now he might be asleep in his chair. Or perhaps he was on the front terrace, peeking through the salon windows at the dancers circling over the polished floor.

But who could there be who hated her enough to try to gas her to death?

With sudden deep dismay, she realized that, even though it had been the farthest thing from her intention, she had quite a few enemies since coming to England. Certainly from this morning on, Sir Rodney would always feel a fear-born hatred of her. Jonathan Burke obviously hated her, not only because she had rebuffed him but also because Martin Cramer, on her account, had threatened to expose his thievery. Diane Olmstead, probably because she suspected Maryann of an interest in Jonathan, had shown unmistakable hostility that day on the train. As for Lady Athaire, she sometimes had vented ill temper upon Maryann, but had manifested nothing that could be called hatred. Still, Maryann could not rule out the possibility that Lady Athaire had somehow found out about her conversation with that stroke-addled man in Liverpool. If so, she too was now harboring a deadly fear that Maryann might reveal to others the long-ago adultery that had produced Jonathan.

For some time now, she had been aware that the faint strains of music below had ceased. So had the sounds of carriages rolling away in the night. Get back to sleep, she told herself. Try!

Somehow she did fall asleep, shortly after the first gray light of a midsummer dawn filled the room. She did not awaken until Agnes, holding a breakfast tray, knocked on her door.

29

She had expected that her employer would reproach her for the previous night's episode. Instead, she was greeted with exuberant chatter about the ball. Plainly her ladyship, despite only a few hours' sleep, was still feeling the elation of the successful hostess. Sir Somebody-or-other had called it the most "brilliant" occasion he had attended in months. And old Lord Deering and his lady, who usually tottered home at eleven o'clock had stayed until two.

Only once did her ladyship mention the gas jet episode, and then only in passing. She had been talking about Diane Olmstead. "I'll admit her gown was lovely, but her face!"

"Her face?"

"Didn't you notice? She was one of those who came up to the landing after you fell down the stairs. Perhaps you were too upset to notice. But anyway, she had a rash on one side of her face! She'd tried to cover it with powder, but of course, with the dancing and all, the powder had worn off."

For Lady Athaire, obviously, Diana's rash only added to the evening's triumph. Looking at her employer's elated face, Maryann found it impossible to imagine her leaving her guests and stealing up to the servants' floor to turn on that gas jet. Spiteful she was, in a childishly gleeful way. But capable of murder? No.

In fact now, with sunlight streaming through the windows—sunlight washed to brilliance by last night's rain—Maryann was suddenly sure that no one had turned on the jet. It had been an accident, one of her own making. Tired and worried, she had reverted to old habit and blown out the flame.

The conviction made her feel foolish. But better, far better, to feel like a fool than like the object of someone's deadly hatred.

Several hours later, when she went up to her rooms for her midday meal, she found a letter on her tray. It bore the postmark of Carlisle, Cumberland. Martin Cramer had said he was going to Cumberland. With not quite steady fingers, she opened his letter.

He had purchased the cattle and arranged for their eventual shipment to a small Texas port called Corpus Christi. He intended to return to Windmere before the end of the week. He hoped that she was well. He remained her "obed. s'v't, Martin Cramer."

Scarcely what one could call a warm letter. But she found it gratifying that he had written at all, absorbed as he must have been by business matters.

Early in the afternoon Lady Athaire's spirits suddenly dropped. After all, as she told Maryann, she had had only three hours' sleep the night before. She would nap until teatime, and her secretary could do whatever she liked.

Gratefully, Maryann went out through the rose garden and turned onto the path that led to the quarry. It was indeed a beautiful day, with lark songs spilling through the air and a few fleecy clouds emphasizing the sky's serene blue. The sunlight and the thirsty earth had caused all but a few small puddles to disappear from the footpath.

She settled herself on the flat rock above the quarry, her knees drawn up under her skirts and her arms wrapped around her legs, when movement caught her eye. Luddy was descending the rough stone steps carved into the quarry's opposite wall. At the water's edge she crouched on the wide bottom step and took off her blouse. She wore nothing under it. While Maryann watched, repelled and yet fascinated, Luddy bent over, her withered breasts dangling, and doused the blouse vigorously up and down in the water.

She was wringing out the cloth when she looked up and spied Maryann. She raised one arm in a friendly wave. Then she turned and began to climb the steps. She had not donned the wet blouse. Instead, still rolled up as when she had finished wringing it, she had placed it around her neck like a scarf. She was walking along the quarry's edge now, still naked to the waist. She sat down beside Maryann.

"Picked up a louse somewhere," she said. "See the bites on my shoulder? Figured I'd better drown the bugger."

In astounded fascination, Maryann stared at the pendulous breasts.

Butterflies. A large blue one tattooed on each breast. Their shape was distorted by the sagging flesh, but they still were indisputably butterflies.

Now Maryann understood the ribald note in her father-in-law's chuckle as he said, "A great one for butterflies, she was."

All along she had found it hard, although not impossible, to believe that a baronet's wife, however humble her origins, had borne the child of a farm-bred worker on the Liverpool docks. But it was not in the least hard to think of Luddy in that role. Oh, not the Luddy of today. The Luddy of a quarter of a century ago or more. A young woman more than a bit daft, but that would not make her any less enjoyable as a partner for a bout of lovemaking in a haystack, or on the bed of a farm wagon, or even in a secluded spot on the open moor.

Luddy shook out her wet blouse, thudded it against the rock's surface a few times, and then put it on. "Ought to dry faster on me." With grimy fingers she did up the buttons. There were only four buttons, although there were more than twice that many buttonholes.

"Luddy."

Luddy looked at her with friendly, squirrel-bright eyes.

"Do you remember a man named Ian Fallon?"

The face in its tangle of graying hair lit up. "Ian! That name I remember. A big man. Purtiest man I ever seen." She cackled. "Got me in the family way, he did."

Maryann's heart was beating hard. No use in asking when it happened. She sensed that to Luddy last month and thirty years ago would be much the same. "Was it a boy or a girl?"

"Boy. Purtiest boy you ever seen. And big, like Ian."

"What became of him?"

"I dunno. Had to leave him beside the road."

So that was how the Burkes had acquired Jonathan. Why hadn't they said so? Perhaps because they *wanted* to believe he was their son. Perhaps because they feared the pain he might feel if ever he learned that he had been abandoned as an infant. (Not that Maryann thought he would have felt pain. Rage, perhaps, but not pain. It might be that the Burkes, though, had not seen aspects of him that others had.) Or there might have been some other, unguessed reason for their silence.

Luddy was speaking. "I pervided for him, though. I wrapped a ring up in his blanket."

"A ring?"

"Big red ring I got off this Aussie bloke in a tavern—" She frowned as if trying to remember the tavern's name, or perhaps where it was, and then said, "He was drunk, this bloke. He took me to bed, and while he was asleep I found the ring in his pocket."

Had the ring been really valuable—Was that why the Burkes had not told the truth? Aloud Maryann asked, "Why did you wrap it up with the baby?"

Suddenly the woman's manner held a touching dignity. "I wanted to pervide for him. Only baby I ever had, except for two what was born dead. I thought whoever picked him up would treat him better when they saw the ring. Must be gentlefolk's baby, they'd think."

Maryann did not point out that gentlefolk, whatever their other shortcomings, were seldom reduced to abandoning their offspring at the roadside. Luddy would not understand, and besides, Maryann's heart at the moment was too full of joyous relief for her to say anything.

Ian Fallon was not the source of the insanity in his younger son. It was this small creature who had passed on the madness—a harmless, childish witlessness in her case, but vicious and dangerous insanity in her son's. And that meant that her own child, James Donald Fallon, had as good as chance as anyone of growing up sound in mind and body.

How swiftly one's life could change! Yesterday at this time she had been weighted with worries and fears. Now her heart soared like one of those larks up there. The fear had vanished as if it had never been, the fear that Jaimie might grow up into another Jonathan.

What was more, Martin had written her a letter and would be home in a few days.

She stood up. "I must go now."

"Got to dry me blouse out a little more," Luddy said. Then: "Spare me tuppence?"

"I wish I had tuppence with me." In fact, she wished she could pour crowns and guineas into the lap of Luddy's soiled skirt.

"Well, happen you'll meet a man. *Then* you'll get tuppence," Luddy said, and added the same obscene pleasantry of days before.

The minister's daughter actually laughed, head thrown back. "Good-bye," she said, and started across the sun-drenched moor toward Windmere.

30

The next day was as lovely as the one before. All that morning she longed to be outdoors and on her way to the quarry. But she found herself even busier than usual. Thank-you missives from ball guests kept arriving at Windmere's entrance, from where they were conveyed to Lady Athaire's rooms. Maryann opened each letter and read it to her gratified employer. In the case of some particularly glowing messages, Lady Athaire asked that they be read twice. Then Maryann placed them in alphabetical order in a long, narrow box covered with green leather.

It was not until three o'clock that Lady Athaire announced that she would take a pre-teatime nap. Free at last, Maryann did not even go upstairs for the headcovering, either a shawl or a bonnet, that decorum decreed any female past young girlhood should wear when out of doors. Instead, she hurried out through the rose garden and took the path to the quarry.

No clouds at all today. Just blue, blue sky, but the larks were there, melody cascading earthward from their throats. High in the heavens a hawk sailed in narrowing circles. She wondered about his quarry. A cowering rabbit? An as yet-oblivious partridge, her feathered breast settled on her nest? One of those singing larks? Then she tried to push the thought of the hawk aside. She would think of Jaimie, growing to healthy manhood. And she would think of Martin Cramer, who might very well be with her by tomorrow at this time.

She reached the quarry. No Luddy today, either clothed or seminaked. The swallows were there, though, wheeling and diving in their pursuit of insects.

She sat down on the flat rock, looked around her. No one in sight. Nor did she have that disquieting sense that had come to her at times here, that feeling that she was being observed. With utter disregard for propriety, she stretched out on the warm rock, hands linked beneath her dark head, eyes closed against the sunlight.

Sometimes, in spite of all the heartbreak and anxiety and hardship, it was good just to be alive, just to feel sunlight, and hear birdsong, and smell heather and grass. Perhaps such intervals did not come often, but they came.

Her thoughts began to drift. Summers in the parsonage back in Connecticut. The swing that her father had made for her. As the swing rose and fell, she had looked up at the silvery undersides of maple leaves moving against the sky. The image of maple leaves blended with that of oak leaves, arching up like little hands above the sidewalk when she came home from school in the fall.

She had almost slid into sleep when she heard a horse nicker.

She opened her eyes, sat up. About a hundred feet away a slender woman in a riding habit was tethering a beautifully groomed chesnut horse to a rowan tree. When the woman turned around, Maryann saw that she was Diane Olmstead.

Maryann started to get to her feet.

"No, no! Don't get up. I thought we might sit and chat for a while." The blond girl dropped her riding crop and then sat down beside it on the flat rock, her legs curled around her under her dark blue velvet skirt.

Maryann too was sitting now, her knees drawn up, her arms wrapped around her legs. She said, bewildered, "What is it you want to talk about?" Irrelevantly, she noticed that if Diane's rash had been real and not just a product of Lady Athaire's wishful imagination, it was gone now.

Diane said coldly, "About whatever it was that dreadful creature told you yesterday."

Maryann said, after a stupefied moment, "Luddy? How is it that you know Luddy was here yesterday?"

"Because I've been having you watched."

It took a moment for Maryann to absorb the words. So there had been a reason for it, that sense of being under observation. Her gaze lifted to one of the low hills surrounding the quarry.

"No, he's not there. I paid him off."

"But why? Why have you had me watched? And for how long?"

"Ever since you got off that train at Marly-on-Willowbrook. You went to see the Burkes about Jonathan, didn't you?"

Looking at the girl's tense white face, Maryann felt a stab of pity. How terrible it must be to love so obsessively when the object of your love was completely unworthy of it.

"Yes."

"Why did you go to see them?"

"Jonathan Burke looks so very much like—like my late husband. I felt they must be half-brothers."

Diane nodded. "I knew you must have had some such bee in your bonnet. Elaine Athaire said you'd told her Jonathan closely resembled someone you'd known in America. You didn't tell her it was your husband, though, did you?" Not waiting for Maryann's reply, she asked, "What did the Burkes tell you?"

"That Jonathan was their natural-born son. I didn't believe them, but that was what they said."

"And what did you learn in Liverpool? The man I hired later learned that there was an Ian Fallon living above that chandler's shop. Your father-in-law, Mrs. Fallon?"

"Yes."

"And what did you learn from him?"

"What I had been almost certain of anyway. That he was Jonathan's father as well as my husband's."

She hesitated. Should she also tell her that until yesterday she had believed Elaine Athaire to be Jonathan's mother? No, she decided. Even though she had banished the idea from her own mind by persuading herself that Lady Athaire and her husband's steward were *not* lovers, she still disliked the memory of those moments when she had wondered if Lady Athaire was guilty not just of adultery but of incestuous adultery. And so why talk of those thoughts she had harbored?

"Well?" Diane prompted. "What else did the old man tell you?"

"Nothing much. You see, he's had a stroke. All I could learn definitely was that he had fathered a child named Jonathan."

Diane's cool gaze was skeptical, but all she said was, "Let's get to the point. What did that creature—Luddy? Is that her name?" Maryann nodded. "What did she tell you yesterday that sent you off acting as if you'd won a million pounds?"

It was worth more than a million pounds, Maryann thought. Then she stopped to consider. Tell the truth to this infatuated girl, this girl perhaps five years younger than herself? Yes, she thought. Then perhaps Diane would manage to root him out of her heart, this man who could bring her only pain and shame and perhaps, ultimately, horror.

"Luddy told me that she was Jonathan's mother."

Impossible to tell whether Diane had harbored even a faint expectation of those words. Her face looked suddenly as cold and hard as marble.

"I don't believe that."

"I do. And I'm sure that anyone skilled in such matters would soon manage to prove it by questioning the Burkes, and my father-in-law, and Luddy herself. Someone might consider such questioning worthwhile. You see, it seems that there was a ring involved, probably an expensive one."

Diane manifested no interest in the ring. Instead she asked, her face still white but her voice steady, "What did Lady Athaire say about all this?"

"Lady Athaire? Why, nothing. I did not tell her about it. Why should I tell anyone?"

Except Martin. As soon as possible she would let him

know that it had vanished, the terrible fear that she had told him about that night in her rooms.

Diane Olmstead said, "Stand up."

Maryann stared at her uncomprehendingly.

"Stand up," Diane repeated and got to her own feet. Still uncomprehending but with cold, growing uneasiness, Maryann also stood up.

"You have told no one," Diane said. "I must keep it that way. In time my father might accept my marrying Jonathan. But never, never, if he knew that foul madwoman—"

Maryann said with sudden comprehension, "Ever since that day on the train, you've been afraid of what I might find out, haven't you? That was why you slipped up to the third floor and turned the gas on in my room."

"Yes. But something or other woke you up."

She reached into the pocket of her riding skirt and brought out a delicate little gun. Pearl handled, with a short, slim barrel, it looked like a toy.

But not for a moment did Maryann think it was. The look in the blond girl's eyes told her that the gun was quite real.

"Perhaps you think *I* am mad, Mrs. Fallon, and that with a few soothing words you can dissuade me. But I am not mad. I just know what I want. I want Jonathan, and neither you nor anyone else will stop me from getting him. Now back up, Mrs. Fallon."

Back up, so that when the girl finally used that dainty little gun, Maryann's body would plummet deep, deep into the quarry water. No doubt the gun would follow her. Then Diane Olmstead would ride away with no betraying blood-stains left on that flat rock.

212

Oh, no, Maryann thought fiercely. Not now, when I've just found out how much there is to live for.

Apparently obedient, Maryann backed one step, two, three. She saw a slender finger tighten on the gun's trigger.

She thought, *Now*, and launched herself forward, bent double. But no bullet sang over her head. All she heard was a click, then another click.

She straightened. Diane, in retreat now, pulled back her arm, flung the little gun.

By wild chance, it struck Maryann's forehead. Half stunned, half blinded by the bright spots dancing in front of her eyes, Maryann staggered several steps.

And then her foot found nothing but air, and she realized that she had moved the wrong way, and that in another split second she would be falling, falling—

Her right leg scraped the cliff's face. Her hands, desperately reaching, grasped the ledge. Her dangling feet with equal desperation sought some outcropping. Her right foot found a protuberance, but after a second or two she could feel it crumbling—

She looked up, saw Diane's face, that lovely face that now, seen from below and contorted with hatred, looked hideous. With the handle of her riding crop, she was beating at Maryann's fingers, which somehow felt nothing at all, even though she knew they must be bruised and torn. The misfiring gun, she thought irrelevantly, must have slithered over the rock into the water. Otherwise Diane would be using it, not the whip handle.

The little outcrop of rock supporting Maryann's right foot gave way.

Her fingers, despite that battering crop handle, clung

even harder. How deep was the quarry's water? One of the servants at Windmere had told her, but whether it was fifty feet or twice that she could not recall. Anyway, it didn't matter. She couldn't swim.

Abruptly, inexplicably, that grimly determined face above her seemed to jerk backward, disappear. In its place another face. Other hands grasping hers, drawing her upward. A hand cupping her left elbow, then her right, and lifting her until she stood groggily on the flat rock.

Martin said, "My God! What happened?"

Dimly she was aware of a sobbing Diane Olmstead, crumpled in the grass at the outer edge of the rock. Suddenly the girl scrambled to her feet, ran toward the chestnut horse tied to a rowan tree. With a hoarse shout, Martin started after her.

Maryann's bruised and bloodied hand caught his arm. "Don't!"

"But she was trying to—"

"I know. But for now, let her go."

In a way, she realized, she was speaking out of selfishness. She was too glad to be alive, too glad to *want* to be alive, to welcome the thought of pursuing criminal charges against that girl, that poor, obsessed girl now riding away. If she ever did manage to marry her Jonathan, she would reap more than adequate punishment for what she had attempted today.

For the first time Maryann saw, through the rowan's wind-stirred leaves, that there was a gray horse tethered to a tree beyond it.

Martin said, "All right. We can decide what to do later. Right now we have to take care of those hands of yours."

214

Maryann knew there was a doctor in the village. But that would mean explanations. "Can't you do it?

"Yes. I've got a medical kit in my rooms."

With his arm supporting her, he led her along the path. He said, "Now, will you please tell me—"

"It was about Jonathan, of course. She feared I'd learned something about his parentage, and I had. His mother was Luddy."

"Luddy!"

"Yes. She told me so herself. Diane was afraid that if her father learned the truth, he would never allow her to marry Jonathan." She paused. "Martin?"

"Yes?"

"I didn't expect you until tomorrow at the earliest."

"I know. But I finished my business a little ahead of time, and I—I found myself eager to get back to Windmere."

He paused. Maryann knew that he, too, was thinking, Thank God for that.

He went on. "Lothar told me when I rode into the stable that he had seen you headed for the quarry, and that in fact you often went there."

They had reached the gray horse now. He said, looking down at her, "There's a bruise on your forehead. I hadn't noticed it until now."

She smiled. "It will go away."

He lifted her onto the gray horse, untethered it, mounted in front of her. She said, arms encircling his waist, "So you are really going to America."

"Yes, when I've completed my arrangements." He paused and then said rapidly, "I was thinking you might want to

215

go to your own country, too. Of course, I realize it is too early for you to consider—an engagement. But I could arrange for us to travel on the same ship. I could stay for a while in that state of yours—what is it called?"

"Connecticut."

"I could stay there until I received word that my cattle have landed in Texas. And perhaps by that time—"

How shy men were, really, and how intimidated by the rules. Her own sex outwardly observed the rules—in fact, insisted upon them. But inwardly, the dreams were given magnificent freedom. In her special dream there was a vast plain where Martin rode among teeming cattle with a tow-headed Jaimie beside him and perhaps, later on, another son with his own dark hair. And at the heart of it all a house where she would prepare a meal for all three of her men—

She said primly, "Yes, I would indeed appreciate it if you looked into possible arrangements for my early return to America."